INTO VIETNAM

SAS
OPERATION

Into Vietnam

SHAUN CLARKE

HARPER

Harper
An imprint of HarperCollins*Publishers*
1 London Bridge Street,
London SE1 9GF
www.harpercollins.co.uk

This paperback edition 2016
1

First published by 22 Books/Bloomsbury Publishing plc 1995

A catalogue record for this book
is available from the British Library

ISBN: 978 0 00 815542 1

Set in Sabon by Born Group using Atomik ePublisher from Easypress

Printed and bound in Great Britain

MIX
Paper from
responsible sources
FSC
www.fsc.org   **FSC C007454**

FSC is a non-profit international organisation established
to promote the responsible management of the world's forests.
Products carrying the FSC label are independently certified
to assure consumers that they come from forests that are managed
to meet the social, economic and ecological needs
of present and future generations.

Find out more about HarperCollins and the environment at
www.harpercollins.co.uk/green

Prelude

The Viet Cong guerrillas emerged from the forest at dawn, with the mist drifting eerily about their heads. There were nearly fifty men, most dressed like coolies in black, pyjama-style combat gear and black felt hats, with sandals or rubber-soled boots on their feet. Nearly all of them were small and frail from lack of nourishment and years of fighting. Their weapons were varied: Soviet-made Kalashnikov AK47 machine-fed 7.62mm assault rifles; 7.62mm RPD light machine-guns with hundred-round link-belt drum magazines; 7.62mm PPS43 sub-machine-guns with a folding metal butt stock and thirty-five-round magazine; Soviet RPG7V short-range, anti-armour, rocket-propelled grenade launchers; and, for the officers only, Soviet Tokarev T33 7.62mm pistols, recoil-operated, semi-automatic and with an eight-round magazine.

As the VC left the forest behind them and crossed the paddy-field, wading ankle deep in water, the officers quietly slid their Tokarevs from their holsters and cocked them.

The Vietnamese hamlet was spread over a broad expanse of dusty earth surrounded by trees and its edge was about fifty yards beyond the paddy-field. With thatched huts, communal latrines, some cultivated plots, a regular supply of

1

food from the nearby paddy-field, and a total of no more than fifty souls, it was exactly what the guerrillas were looking for.

Though this was an agricultural hamlet, the VC had been informed that the peasants had been trained by the CIA's Combined Studies Division and Australian Special Air Service (SAS) teams in hamlet defence, including weapon training, moat and palisade construction, ambushing and setting booby-traps. The peasants were being armed and trained by the Americans in the hope that they would protect themselves against guerrilla attacks. What had been happening in practice, however, is that the VC, more experienced and in much greater numbers, had been destroying such hamlets and using the captured American arms and supplies against American and South Vietnamese forces elsewhere.

This was about to happen again.

The first to spot the VC were two peasants working at the far edge of the paddy-field. One of them glanced up, saw the raiding party and hastily waded out of the paddy-field and ran back to the hamlet. The second man was just about to flee when one of the VC officers fired at the first with his Tokarev.

The sound of that single shot was shockingly loud in the morning's silence, making birds scatter from the trees to the sky, chickens squawk in panic, and dogs bark with the false courage of fear.

The 7.62mm bullet hit the man's lower body, just beside the spinal column, violently punching him forward. Even as the first man was splashing face down in the water, the other man was rushing past him to get to dry land and the villagers were looking up in surprise. He had just reached the dry earth at the edge of the paddy-field when several VC fired at him with their AK47s, making him shudder like a rag doll, tearing him to shreds, then hurling him to the ground as the dust billowed up all around him.

A woman in the hamlet let out a long, piercing scream as the wounded man managed to make it to his knees, coughing water and blood from his lungs. Even as he was waving his arms frantically to correct his balance, pistols and assault rifles roared together. When he plunged backwards into the paddy-field, his clothes lacerated, the bullet holes pumping blood, wails of dread and despair arose from the hamlet.

While the women gathered their children around them and ushered them into the thatched houses, the men trained by the Americans rushed to take up positions in the defensive slit trenches armed with 7.62mm M60 GPMGs – general-purpose machine-guns. Others rushed to their thatched huts and emerged carrying L1A1 SLR semi-automatic rifles of the same calibre as the machine-guns. They threw themselves on the ground overlooking the moat filled with lethal punji stakes and wooden palisades constructed by Australian SAS troops, taking aim at the attackers. The VC were now emerging from the paddy-field and marching directly towards the minefield that encircled the hamlet.

Abruptly, the VC, who knew that the village was part of the US Strategic Hamlet Program and therefore well protected, split into three groups, two of which circled around the village, weaving through the palm trees just beyond the minefield. As they were doing so, the third group were taking positions in a hollow at the far side of the moat, between the paddy-field and the hamlet, and there setting up two Chinese 60mm mortars.

Realizing with horror that the two VC groups could only be circling around the back of the hamlet because they knew the location of the patrol route exit through the minefield;

3

and that they were also going to mortar-bomb a way through the minefield at the front – information they must have obtained from an informer – some of the villagers opened fire with their rifles and GPMGs as others raced back across the clearing to stop the guerrillas getting in. This second group was, however, badly decimated when a third VC mortar fired half a dozen shells in quick succession, blowing the running men apart and then exploding in a broad arc that took in some of the surrounding thatched huts and set them ablaze.

As the flames burst ferociously from the thatched roofs and the wailing of women and children was heard from within, the first mortar shells aimed at the minefield exploded with a deafening roar. Soil, dust and smoke spewed skyward and then spread out to obscure the VC as some of them stood up and advanced at the crouch to the edge of the mined area. Kneeling there and checking where the mortars had exploded, the guerrillas saw that they nearly had a clear path and could complete the job with another few rounds.

Using hand signals, the leader of this group indicated a slightly lower elevation, then dropped to the ground as a hail of gunfire came from the frantic villagers at the other side of the minefield. When the second round of mortar shells had exploded, throwing up more billowing smoke and dust, the first of the VC advanced along the path of charred holes created by the explosions. That crudely cleared route led them safely through the minefield and up to the edge of the moat, where some of them were chopped down by the villagers' guns and the rest threw themselves to the ground to return fire.

By now the other two groups of VC had managed to circle around to the back of the hamlet and, using the map given to them by the informer, had located the patrol route exit and started moving carefully along it in single file. Almost instantly, the first of them were cut down by the few armed peasants who had managed to escape the mortars exploding in the centre of the hamlet. As the first of the VC fell, however, the rest opened fire with their AK47s, felling the few peasants who had managed to get this far. The rest of the guerrillas then raced along the patrol route exit, into the centre of the hamlet, where, with the screams and weeping of women and children in their ears, they were able to come up behind the villagers defending the moat to the front.

Some of the women kneeling in the clearing in front of their burning homes cried out warnings to their men, but it was too late. Caught in a withering crossfire from front and rear, the villagers firing across the moat, among them a few teenage girls, were chopped to pieces and died screaming and writhing in a convulsion of spewing soil and dust. Those who did not die immediately were put to death by the bayonet. When their mothers, wives or children tried to stop this, they too were dispatched in the same way. Within minutes the attack was over and the remaining VC were wading across the moat and clambering up to the clearing.

In a state of shock and grief, and surrounded by their dead relatives and friends, the rest of the villagers were easily subdued and forced to kneel in the middle of the clearing. The remaining thatched huts were then searched by the guerrillas and those inside prodded out at bayonet or gun point. After a rigorous interrogation – faces were slapped and lots of insults were shouted, though no other form of torture was used – the villagers considered to be 'traitors' to the communists were led away and made to kneel by the moat. There they were shot, each with a single bullet to the back of the head, then their bodies were kicked over the edge into the water.

When this grisly operation was over, the rest of the villagers, many in severe shock, were forced into separate work groups. One of these, composed only of men and teenage boys, was made to drag the dead bodies out of the moat with meat-hooks, then place them on ox carts and take them to a cleared area just outside the perimeter, where they were buried without ceremony in a shallow pit.

When, about three hours later, this work party, now exhausted and in an even worse state of shock, returned to the hamlet, they found their friends already at work clearing away the burnt-out dwellings and unwanted foliage with machetes, hoes, short-handled spades and buckets under the impassive but watchful gaze of armed VC guards. Assigned their individual tasks in this joint effort, they began with the others what would be weeks of hard, nightmarish, ingenious work: the construction of an elaborate tunnel system directly under the devastated hamlet.

First, a series of large, rectangular pits, each about fifteen feet deep, was dug on the sites of the destroyed huts. Over these pits were raised sloping thatched roofs of the type found on the other dwellings, though the newly built roofs were mere inches off the ground. Viewed from the air, they would suggest normal hamlet houses.

Once the thatched roofs had been raised, work began on digging a series of tunnels leading down from the floor of each pit. Most of these were so narrow that there was only enough space for a single, slim body to wriggle along them, and in places they descended vertically, like a well, before continuing at a gentler slope in one direction or another. The only tunnel not beginning in one of the pits and not making any kind of bend was a well, its water table about forty feet deep and its surface access, level with the ground, camouflaged with a web of bamboo covered with soil and shrubbery.

One of the pits served as a kitchen, complete with bamboo shelves and a stone-walled stove. Smoke was vented into a pipe that spewed it into a tunnel running about eight feet underground until it was 150 feet west of the kitchen, where it emerged through three vents hidden in the palm trees beyond the perimeter.

An escape tunnel descended from the floor of the kitchen, curving west and crossing two concealed trapdoors before dividing into two even narrower tunnels. One of these was a false tunnel that led to a dead end; the other, concealed, rose steeply until it reached an escape hole hidden in the trees beyond the smoke outlets. A third escape tunnel, hidden by a concealed trapdoor, led away from the tunnel complex but linked up with another under the next village to the west. Of the other two trapdoors in this escape route, one had to be skirted, as the weight of a human body would make it collapse and drop that person to a hideous death in a trap filled with poisoned punji stakes. The third concealed trapdoor ran down into a large cavern hacked out of the earth about thirty feet down, to be used as a storage area for weapons, explosives and rice.

A short tunnel running east from the entrance to the underground storage area led into the middle of the well, about halfway down. On the opposite side of the well, but slightly lower, where the man pulling water up with a bucket and rope could straddle both ledges with his feet, another tunnel curved up and levelled out. At that point there was another trapdoor, and this covered a tunnel that climbed vertically to the floor of a conical air-raid shelter, so shaped because it amplified the sound of approaching aircraft and therefore acted as a useful warning system.

Leading off the air-raid shelter was another tunnel curving vertically until it reached the conference chamber. Complete with long table, wooden chairs and blackboard, the conference chamber was located in another of the pits, under a thatched roof almost touching the ground.

A narrow airing tunnel led from the pyramidal roof of the air-raid shelter to the surface; another led down to where the tunnel below levelled out and ran on to a second dead end, but one with another trapdoor in the floor. This trapdoor, proof against blast, gas and water, covered a tunnel that dropped straight down before curving around and up again in a series of loops that formed a natural blast wall. The top of this tunnel was sealed off by a second, similarly protective trapdoor, located in another cavernous area hacked out of the earth about fifteen feet down.

Though this cavernous area was empty – its only purpose to allow gas to dissipate and water to drain away – a series of interlinking access and exit tunnels ran off it. One led even deeper, to a large, rectangular space that would be used as the forward aid station for the wounded. The escape tunnel leading from this chamber ran horizontally under the ground, about twenty-five feet down, parallel to the surface, until it reached the similar network of tunnels under the next hamlet to the east.

The tunnel ascending to the east of the empty cavern led to another concealed trapdoor and two paths running in opposite directions: one to a camouflaged escape hole, the other to another pit dug out of the ground, this one not covered with a decoy thatched roof, but camouflaged with foliage and used as a firing post for both personal and anti-aircraft weapons.

West of this firing post, and similarly camouflaged, was a ventilation shaft running obliquely down to the empty cavern over the tunnel trap used as a natural blast wall. West of this ventilation shaft was the first of a series of punji pits, all camouflaged. West of the first punji pit was another concealed, ground-level trapdoor entrance that led into another tunnel descending almost vertically to a further hidden trapdoor.

Anyone crawling on to this last trapdoor would find it giving way beneath them and pitching them to their death on the sharpened punji stakes below. However, anyone skirting the trapdoor and crawling on would reach the biggest chamber of them all – the VCs' sleeping and living quarters, with hammock beds, folding chairs and tables, stone chamber pots, bamboo shelves for weapons and other personal belongings, and all the other items that enable men to live for long periods like rats underground.

After weeks of hard labour by both South Vietnamese peasants and VC soldiers, this vast complex of underground tunnels was complete and some of the peasants were sent above ground to act as if the hamlet were running normally. Though still in a state of shock at the loss of friends, relatives and livelihood, the peasants knew that they were being watched all the time and would be shot if they made the slightest protest or tried to warn those defending South Vietnam.

Those peasants still slaving away in the tunnel complex would remain there to complete what would become in time four separate levels similar to the one they had just constructed. The levels would be connected by an intricate network of passages, some as narrow as eighty centimetres, with ventilation holes that ran obliquely to prevent monsoon rain flooding and were orientated so as to catch the morning light and bring in fresh air from the prevailing easterly winds.

The guerrillas not watching the peasants were living deep underground, existing on practically nothing, constantly smelling the stench of their own piss and shit, emerging from the fetid chambers and dank tunnels only when ordered to go out and strike down the enemy. Like trapdoor spiders, they saw the light of day only when they brought the darkness of death.

1

The swamp was dark, humid, foul-smelling and treacherous. Wading chest deep in the scum-covered water, Sergeant Sam 'Shagger' Bannerman and his sidekick, Corporal Tom 'Red' Swanson, both holding their jungle-camouflaged 7.62mm L1A1 self-loading rifles above their heads, were being assailed by mosquitoes, stinging hornets and countless other crazed insects. After slogging through the jungle for five days, they were both covered in bruises and puss-filled stings and cuts, all of which drove the blood lust of their attackers to an even greater pitch.

'You try to talk . . .' Red began, then, almost choking on an insect, coughed and spat noisily in an attempt to clear his throat. 'You try to talk and these bloody insects fly straight into your mouth. Jesus Christ, this is terrible!'

'No worse than Borneo,' Sergeant Bannerman replied. 'Well, maybe a little . . .'

In fact, it was worse. Shagger had served with 1 Squadron SAS (Australian Special Air Service) of Headquarters Far East Land Forces during the Malaya Emergency in 1963. In August of that year he had joined the Training Team in Vietnam, and from February to October 1964 had been with the first Australian team to operate with the US Special Forces at

Nha Trang. Then, in February 1966, he was posted with 1 Squadron SAS to Sarawak, Borneo, and spent two months there before being recalled, along with a good half of 1 Squadron, to the SAS headquarters at Swanbourne, Perth, for subsequent transfer to 3 Squadron SAS, training especially for the new Task Force in Vietnam. They had not yet reached 'Nam, but would certainly be there soon, once they had completed this business in the hell of New Guinea. Shagger had indeed seen it all – and still he thought this was bad.

'Not much longer to go,' he said, still wading waist deep in the sludge and finding it difficult because the bed of the swamp was soft and yielding, being mainly a combination of mud and small stones but dangerously cluttered with larger stones, fallen branches and other debris. The task of wading on this soft bottom was not eased by the fact that Shagger and Red were both humping 90lb of bergen rucksack and 11lb of loaded SLR semiautomatic assault rifle. The problems were further compounded by the knowledge that the surface of the water was covered with a foul-smelling slime composed of rotted seeds, leaves and moss. It was also cluttered with obstructions that included giant razor-edged palm leaves and floating branches, the latter hard to distinguish from the highly venomous sea-snakes that infested the place. If these weren't bad enough, there were other snakes in the branches that overhung the swamp, brushing the men's heads, as well as poisonous spiders and bloodsucking leeches. So far, while neither soldier had been bitten by a venomous sea-snake or spider, both had lost a lot of blood to the many leeches that attached themselves to their skin under the water or after falling from the branches or palm leaves above them.

'My eyes are all swollen,' Red complained. 'I can hardly see a thing.'

'Your lips are all swollen as well,' Shagger replied, 'but you still manage to talk.'

'I'm just trying to keep your pecker up, Sarge.'

'With whinges and moans? Just belt up and keep wading. We'll get there any moment now and then you can do a bit of spine bashing' – he meant have a rest – 'and tend to your eyes and other swollen parts, including your balls – if you've got any, that is.'

'I don't remember,' Red said with feeling. 'My memory doesn't stretch back that far.' He had served with Shagger in Borneo, and formed a solid friendship that included a lot of banter. He felt easy with the man. But then, having a philosophical disposition, he rubbed along with most people. 'Actually,' he said, noticing with gratitude that the water was now below his waist, which meant they were moving up on to higher ground, 'I prefer this to Borneo, Sarge. I couldn't stand the bridges in that country. No head for heights, me.'

'You did all right,' Shagger said.

In fact, Red had been terrific. Of all the many terrifying aspects of the campaign in Borneo, the worst was crossing the swaying walkways that spanned the wide and deep gorges with rapids boiling through bottlenecks formed by rock outcroppings hundreds of feet below. Just as in New Guinea, the jungles of Borneo had been infested with snakes, lizards, leeches, wild pigs, all kinds of poisonous insects, and even head-hunters, making it a particularly nightmarish place to fight a war. And yet neither snakes nor head-hunters were a match for the dizzying aerial walkways when it came to striking terror into even the most courageous men.

The walkways were crude bridges consisting of three lengths of thick bamboo laid side by side and strapped together with rattan – hardly much wider than two human feet placed close

13

together. The uprights angled out and in again overhead, and were strapped with rattan to the horizontal holds. You could slide your hands along the holds only as far as the next upright. Once there, you had to remove your hand for a moment and lift it over the upright before grabbing the horizontal hold. All the time you were doing this, inching forward perhaps 150 feet above a roaring torrent, the narrow walkway was creaking and swinging dangerously in the wind that swept along the gorge. It was like walking in thin air.

Even worse, the Australians often had to use the walkways when they were making their way back from a jungle patrol and being pursued by Indonesian troops. At such times the enemy could use the walkways as shooting galleries in which the Aussies made highly visible targets as they inched their way across.

This had been the experience of Shagger and Red during their last patrol before returning to Perth. Their patrol had been caught in the middle of an unusually high walkway, swaying over rapids 160 feet below, while the Indonesians unleashed small-arms fire on them, killing and wounding many men, until eventually they shot the rattan binding to pieces, making the walkway, with some unfortunates still on it, tear away from its moorings, sending the men still clinging to it screaming to their doom.

Shagger, though more experienced than Red, had suffered nightmares about that incident for weeks after the event, but Red, with his characteristic detachment, had only once expressed regret at the loss of his mates and then put the awful business behind him. And though, as he claimed, he had no head for heights, he had been very courageous on the walkways, often turning back to help more frightened men across, even in the face of enemy fire. He was a good man to have around.

14

'The ground's getting higher,' Shagger said, having noticed that the scummy water was now only as high as his knees. 'That means we're heading towards the islet marked on the map. That's our ambush position.'

'You think we'll get there before they do?' Red asked.

'Let us pray,' Shagger replied.

As he waded the last few hundred yards to the islet, now visible as a mound of firm ground covered with seedlings and brown leaves, with a couple of palm trees in the middle, Shagger felt the exhaustion of the past five days falling upon him. Three Squadron SAS had been sent to New Guinea to deploy patrols through forward airfields by helicopter and light aircraft; to patrol and navigate through tropical jungle and mountain terrain; to practise communications and resupply; and to liaise with the indigenous people.

For the past five days, therefore, the SAS men had sweated in the tropical heat; hacked their way through seemingly impassable secondary jungle with machetes; climbed incredibly steep, tree-covered hills; waded across rivers flowing at torrential speeds; oared themselves along slower rivers on 'gripper bar' rafts made from logs and four stakes; slept in shallow, water-filled scrapes under inadequate ponchos in fiercely driving, tropical rainstorms; suffered the constant buzzing, whining and biting of mosquitoes and hornets; frozen as poisonous snakes slithered across their booted feet; lost enormous amounts of blood to leeches; had some hair-raising confrontations with head-hunting natives – and all while reconnoitring the land, noting points of strategic value, and either pursuing, or being pursued by, the enemy.

Now, on the last day, Shagger and Red, having been separated accidentally from the rest of their troop during a shoot-out with an enemy column, were making their way to the location originally chosen for their own troop as an ambush position, where they hoped to have a final victory and then get back to base and ultimately Australia. After their long, arduous hike through the swamp they were both exhausted.

'I'm absolutely bloody shagged,' Red said, gasping. 'I can hardly move a muscle.'

'We can take a rest in a minute,' Shagger told him. 'Here's our home from home, mate. The ambush position.'

The islet was about fifty yards from the far edge of the swamp they had just crossed, almost directly facing a narrow track that snaked into the jungle, curving away out of sight. It was along that barely distinguishable track that the enemy would approach on their route across the swamp, but in the opposite direction as they searched for Shagger's divided patrol, which had undoubtedly been sighted by one of their many reconnaissance helicopters.

Wading up to the islet, pushing aside the gigantic, bright-green palm leaves that floated on its miasmal surface, Shagger and Red finally found firm ground beneath them and were able to lay down their SLRs and shrug off their heavy bergens. Relieved of that weight, they clambered up on to the islet's bed of brown leaves and seedlings, rolled on to their backs and gulped in lungfuls of air. Both men did a lot of deep breathing before talking again.

'Either I'm gonna flake out,' Red finally gasped, 'or I'm gonna have a good chunder. I feel sick with exhaustion.'

'You can't sleep and you can't chuck up,' Shagger told him. 'You can chunder when you get back to base and have a skinful of beer. You can sleep there as well. Right now, though, we have to dig in and set up, then spring our little surprise. Those dills, if they get here at all, will be here before last light, so we have to be ready.'

'Just let me have some water', Red replied, 'and I'll be back on the ball.'

'Go on, mate. Then let's get rid of these bloody leeches and prepare the ambush. We'll win this one, Red.'

When they had quenched their thirst, surprising themselves by doing so without vomiting, they lit cigarettes, inhaled luxuriously for a few minutes, then proceeded to burn off, with their cigarettes, the leeches still clinging to their bruised and scarred skin. As they were both covered with fat, black leeches, all still sucking blood, this operation took several cigarettes. When they had got rid of the bloodsuckers they wiped their skins down with antiseptic cream and set about making a temporary hide.

The islet was an almost perfect circle hardly more than thirty feet in diameter. The thick trees soaring up from the carpet of seedlings and leaves were surrounded by a convenient mass of dense foliage over which the branches draped their gigantic palm leaves. As this natural camouflage would give good protection, Shagger chose this area for the location of the hide and he and Red then dug out two shallow lying-up positions, or LUPs, using the small spades clipped to their webbing.

This done, each man began to construct a simple shelter over his LUP by driving two V-shaped wooden uprights into the soft soil, placed about six feet apart. A length of nylon cord was tied between the uprights, then a waterproof poncho was draped over the cord with the long end facing the prevailing wind and the short, exposed end, facing the path at the far side of the swamp. The two corners of each end were jerked tight and held down with small wooden pegs and nylon cord. The LUP was then filled with a soft bed of leaves and seedlings, a sleeping-bag was rolled out on to it, and the triangular tent was carefully camouflaged with giant leaves and other foliage held down with fine netting.

Once the shelters had been completed, the hide blended in perfectly with the surrounding vegetation, making it practically invisible to anyone coming along the jungle track leading to the swamp.

'If they come out of there,' Shagger said with satisfaction, 'they won't have a prayer. Now let's check our kit.'

The afternoon sun was still high in the sky when each man checked his SLR, removing the mud, twigs, leaves and even cobwebs that had got into it; oiling the bolt, trigger mechanism and other moving parts; then rewrapping it in its jungle-coloured camouflage material. Satisfied that the weapons were in working order, they ate a cold meal of tinned sardines, biscuits and water, battling every second to keep off the attacking insects. Knowing that the enemy trying to find them would attempt to cross the swamp before the sun had set – which meant that if they came at all, they would be coming along the track quite soon – they lay on their bellies in their LUPs, sprinkled more loose foliage over themselves as best they could, and laid the SLRs on the lip of their shallow scrapes, barrels facing the swamp. Then they waited.

'It's been a long five days,' Shagger said.

'Too bloody long,' Red replied. 'And made no better by the fact that we're doing the whole thing on a shoestring. Piss-poor, if you ask me.'

Shagger grinned. 'The lower ranks' whinge. How do you, a no-hoper corporal, know this was done on a shoestring?'

'Well, no RAAF support, for a start. Just that bloody Ansett-MAL Caribou that was completely unreliable . . .'

'Serviceability problems,' Shagger interjected, still grinning. 'But the Trans Australian Airlines DC3s and the Crowley

Airlines G13 choppers were reliable. They made up for the lack of RAAF support, didn't they?'

'You're joking. Those fucking G13s had no winch and little lift capability. They were as useless as lead balloons.'

'That's true,' Shagger murmured, recalling the cumbersome helicopters hovering over the canopy of the trees, whipping up dust and leaves, as they dropped supplies or lifted men out. He fell silent, never once removing his searching gaze from the darkening path that led from the jungle to the edge of the swamp. Then he said, 'They were piss-poor for resups and lift-offs – that's true enough. But the DC3s were OK.'

Red sighed loudly, as if short of breath. 'That's my whole point. This was supposed to be an important exercise, preparing us for 'Nam, and yet we didn't even get RAAF support. Those bastards in Canberra are playing silly buggers and wasting our time.'

'No,' Shagger replied firmly. 'We didn't waste our time. They might have fucked up, but we've learnt an awful lot in these five days and I think it'll stand us in good stead once we go in-country.'

'Let's hope so, Sarge.'

'Anyway, it's no good farting against thunder, so you might as well forget it. If we pull off this ambush we'll have won, then it's spine-bashing time. We can . . .'

Suddenly Shagger raised his right hand to silence Red. At first he thought he was mistaken, but then, when he listened more intently, he heard what he assumed was the distant snapping of twigs and large, hardened leaves as a body of men advanced along the jungle path, heading for the swamp.

Using a hand signal, Shagger indicated to Red that he should adapt the firing position. When Red had done so, Shagger signalled that they should aim their fire in opposite directions, forming a triangular arc that would put a line of bullets through the front and rear of the file of enemy troops when it extended into the swamp from its muddy edge at the end of the path.

As they lay there waiting, squinting along their rifle sights, their biggest problems were ignoring the sweat that dripped from their foreheads into their eyes, and the insects that whined and buzzed about them, driven into a feeding frenzy by the smell of the sweat. In short, the most difficult thing was remaining dead still to ensure that they were not detected by their quarry.

Luckily, just as both of them were thinking that they might be driven mad by the insects, the first of the enemy appeared around the bend in the darkening path. They were marching in the classic single-file formation, with one man out ahead on 'point' as the lead scout, covering an arc of fire immediately in front of the patrol, and the others strung out behind him, covering arcs to the left and right.

When all the members of the patrol had come into view around the bed in the path, with 'Tail-end Charlie' well behind the others, covering an arc of fire to the rear, Shagger counted a total of eight men: two four-man patrols combined. All of them were wearing olive-green, long-sleeved cotton shirts; matching trousers with a drawcord waist; soft jungle hats with a sweat-band around the forehead; and rubber-soled canvas boots. Like Shagger and Red, they were armed with 7.62mm L1A1 SLRs and had 9mm Browning High Power pistols and machetes strung from their waist belts.

In short, the 'enemy' was a patrol of Australian troops.

'Got the buggers!' Shagger whispered, then aimed at the head of the single file as Red was taking aim at its rear. When the last man had stepped into the water, Shagger and Red both opened fire with their SLRs.

Having switched to automatic they stitched lines of spurting water across the front and rear of the patrol. Shocked, but quickly realizing that they were boxed in, the men under attack bawled panicky, conflicting instructions at one another, then split into two groups. These started heading off in opposite directions: one directly towards the islet, the other away from it.

Instantly, Shagger and Red jumped up to lob American M26 hand-grenades, one out in front of the men wading away from the islet, the other in front of the men wading towards it. Both grenades exploded with a muffled roar that threw up spiralling columns of water and rotting vegetation which then rained back down on the fleeing soldiers. Turning back towards one another, the two groups hesitated, then tried to head back to the jungle. They had only managed a few steps when Shagger and Red riddled the shore with the awesome automatic fire of their combined SLRs, tearing the foliage to shreds and showering the fleeing troops with flying branches and dangerously sharp palm leaves.

When the 'enemy' bunched up again, hesitating, Shagger and Bannerman stopped firing.

'Drop your weapons and put your hands in the air!' Shagger bawled at them. 'We'll take that as surrender.'

The men in the water were silent for some time, glancing indecisively at one another; but eventually a sergeant, obviously the platoon leader, cried out: 'Bloody hell!' Then he dropped his SLR into the water and raised both hands. 'Got us fair and square,' he said to the rest of his men. 'We're all prisoners of war. So drop your weapons and put up your hands, you happy wankers. We've lost. Those bastards have won.'

'Too right, we have,' Shagger and Red said simultaneously, with big, cheesy grins.

They had other reasons for smiling. This was the final action in the month-long training exercise 'Traiim Nau', conducted by Australian troops in the jungles and swamps of New Guinea in the spring of 1966.

In June that year, after they had returned to their headquarters in Swanbourne, and enjoyed two weeks' leave, the men of 3 Squadron SAS embarked by boat and plane from Perth to help set up a Forward Operating Base (FOB) in Phuoc Tuy province, Vietnam.

2

In a small, relatively barren room in 'the Kremlin', the Operations Planning and Intelligence section, at Bradbury Lines, Hereford, the Commanding Officer of D Squadron, SAS, Lieutenant-Colonel Patrick 'Paddy' Callaghan, was conducting a most unusual briefing – unusual because there were only two other men present: Sergeants Jimmy 'Jimbo' Ashman and Richard 'Dead-eye Dick' Parker.

Ashman was an old hand who had served with the Regiment since it was formed in North Africa in 1941, fought with it as recently as 1964, in Aden, and now, in his mid-forties, was being given his next-to-last active role before being transferred to the Training Wing as a member of the Directing Staff. Parker had previously fought with the SAS in Malaya and Borneo and alongside Ashman in Aden. Jimbo was one of the most experienced and popular men in the Regiment, while Dead-eye, as he was usually known, was one of the most admired and feared. By his own choice, he had very few friends.

Lieutenant-Colonel Callaghan knew them both well, particularly Jimbo, with whom he went back as far as 1941 when they had both taken part in the Regiment's first forays against the Germans with the Long Range Desert Group.

Under normal circumstances officers could remain with the Regiment for no more than three years at a time. However, they could return for a similar period after a break, and Callaghan, who was devoted to the SAS, had been tenacious in doing just that. For this reason, he had an illustrious reputation based on unparalleled experience with the Regiment. At the end of the war, when the SAS was disbanded, Callaghan had returned to his original regiment, 3 Commando. But when he heard that the SAS was being reformed to deal with the Emergency in Malaya, he applied immediately and was accepted, and soon found himself involved in intense jungle warfare.

After Malaya, Callaghan was returned to Bradbury Lines, then still located at Merebrook Camp, Malvern, where he had worked with his former Malayan Squadron Commander, Lieutenant-Colonel Pryce-Jones, on the structuring of the rigorous new Selection and Training Programme for the Regiment, based mostly on ideas devised and thoroughly tested in Malaya. Promoted to the rank of major in 1962, shortly after the SAS had transferred to Bradbury Lines, Callaghan was returned once again to his original unit, 3 Commando, but then wangled his way back into the SAS, where he had been offered the leadership of D Squadron just before its assignment to the Borneo campaign in 1964.

Shortly after the successful completion of that campaign, when he had returned with the rest of the squadron to Bradbury Lines, he was returned yet again to 3 Commando, promoted once more, then informed that he was now too old for active service and was therefore being assigned a desk job in 'the Kremlin'. Realizing that the time had come to accept the inevitable, he had settled into his new position and was, as ever, working conscientiously when, to his surprise, he was offered the chance to transfer back to the SAS for what the Officer Commanding had emphasized would be his 'absolutely final three-year stint'. Unable to resist the call, Callaghan had turned up at Bradbury Lines to learn that he was being sent to Vietnam.

'This is not a combatant role,' the OC informed him, trying to keep a straight face. 'You'll be there purely in an advisory capacity and – may I make it clear from the outset – in an *unofficial* capacity. Is that understood?'

'Absolutely, sir.'

Though Callaghan was now officially too old to take part in combat, he had no intention of avoiding it should the opportunity to leap in present itself. Also, he knew – and knew that his OC knew it as well – that if he was in Vietnam unofficially, his presence there would be denied and any actions undertaken by him likewise denied. Callaghan was happy.

'This is top-secret,' Callaghan now told Jimbo and Dead-eye from his hard wooden chair in front of a blackboard covered by a black cloth. 'We three – and we three alone – are off to advise the Aussie SAS in Phuoc Tuy province, Vietnam.'

Jimbo gave a low whistle, but otherwise kept his thoughts to himself for now.

'Where exactly is Phuoc Tuy?' Dead-eye asked.

'South-east of Saigon,' Callaghan informed him. 'A swampy hell of jungle and paddy-fields. The VC main forces units have a series of bases in the jungle and the political cadres have control of the villages. Where they don't have that kind of control, they ruthlessly eliminate those communities. The Aussies' job is to stop them.'

'I didn't even know the Aussies were there,' Jimbo said, voicing a common misconception.

'Oh, they're there, all right – and have been, in various guises, for some time. In the beginning, back in 1962, when they were known as the Australian Army Training Team Vietnam – 'the Team' for short – they were there solely to train South Vietnamese units in jungle warfare, village security and related activities such as engineering and signals. Unlike the Yanks, they weren't even allowed to accompany the locals in action against the North Vietnamese, let alone engage in combat.

'Also, the Aussies and Americans reacted to the war in different ways. The Yanks were training the South Vietnamese to combat a massed invasion by North Vietnam across the Demilitarized Zone, established in 1954 under the Geneva Accords, which temporarily divided North Vietnam from South Vietnam along the 17th Parallel. The Americans stressed the rapid development of large forces and the concentration of artillery and air power to deliver a massive volume of fire over a wide area. The Aussies, on the other hand, having perfected small-scale, counter-insurgency tactics, had more faith in those and continued to use them in Vietnam, concentrating on map reading and navigation, marksmanship, stealth, constant patrolling, tracking the enemy and, of course, patience. Much of this they learnt from us back in Malaya during the fifties.'

'That's why they're bloody good,' Jimbo said.

'Don't let them hear you say that,' Dead-eye told him, offering one of his rare, bleak smiles. 'They might not be amused.'

'If they learnt from us, sir, they're good and that's all there is to it.'

'Let me give you some useful background,' Callaghan said. 'Back in 1962, before heading off to Vietnam, the Aussie SAS followed a crash training programme. First, there was a two-week briefing on the war at the Intelligence Centre in Sydney. Then the unit spent five days undergoing intensive jungle-warfare training in Queensland. In early August of that year, with their training completed, twenty-nine SAS men took a regular commercial flight from Singapore to Saigon, all wearing civilian clothing. They changed into the jungle-green combat uniform of the Australian soldier during the flight.'

'In other words, they went secretly,' Dead-eye said.

'Correct. On arrival at Saigon's Tan Son Nhut airport, they were split up into two separate teams. A unit of ten men was sent to Vietnamese National Training Centre at Dong Da, just south of Hue, the old imperial capital. That camp was responsible for the training of recruits for the Army of the Republic of Vietnam, the ARVN, but the base was also used as a battalion training centre and could accommodate about a thousand men. There, though constantly handicapped by the almost total corruption of the ARVN officers, they managed to train recruits and replacements for the regular ARVN Ranger units.

'The second unit, consisting of a group of ten, was sent to the Civil Guard Training Centre at Hiep Kanh, north-west of Hue. The function of the Civil Guard was to protect key points in the provinces – bridges, telephone exchanges, radio stations and various government buildings. Though they weren't nearly as corrupt and undisciplined as the troops of the ARVN, they were considered to be the poor relations, given clapped-out weapons and minimal supplies, then thrown repeatedly against the VC – invariably receiving a severe beating.

'However, shortly after the arrival of the Aussie SAS, most of the Yanks were withdrawn and the Aussies undertook the training of the Vietnamese – a job they carried out very well, it must be said. But as the general military situation in South Vietnam continued to deteriorate, VC pressure on the districts around Hiep Kanh began to increase and in November '63 the camp was closed and the remaining four Aussie advisers were transferred into the US Special Forces – the Ranger Training Centre at Due My, to be precise – some thirty miles inland from Nha Trang.'

'They went there for further training?' Jimbo asked.

'Yes. I'm telling you all this to let you know just how good these guys are. At the Ranger Training Centre there were four training camps: the Base Camp and three specialized facilities – the Swamp Camp, the Mountain Camp and the Jungle Camp – for training in the techniques of fighting in those terrains. Reportedly, however, the men found this experience increasingly frustrating – mainly because they knew that a guerrilla war was being fought all around them, but they still weren't allowed to take part in it.'

'That would drive *me* barmy,' Jimbo said. 'It's the worst bind of all.'

Dead-eye nodded his agreement.

'Other team members,' Callaghan continued, 'were posted to Da Nang to join the CIA's Combined Studies Division, which was engaged in training village militia, border forces and trail-watchers. Two of those Aussie SAS officers had the unenviable task of teaching Vietnamese peasants the techniques of village defence – weapon training, ambushing and booby-traps, and moat and palisade construction. The peasants were transported from their own villages, equipped and trained at Hoa Cam, on the outskirts of Da Nang, then sent back to defend their own homes. Unfortunately, this failed to work and, indeed, inadvertently fed weapons and supplies to the enemy. By this I mean that once they heard what was going on, the VC, who vastly outnumbered the South Vietnamese villagers, simply marched in, took over the villages, and seized the American arms and supplies for use against US and South Vietnamese forces.'

'A bloody farce,' Jimbo said.

'And frustrating too. If the Aussies weren't being driven mad by the corruption and incompetence of the ARVN officers, they were getting screwed by the South Vietnamese government, which bent according to the way the wind blew. For instance, one of the best men the Aussies had out there was Captain Barry Petersen, a veteran of the Malayan counter-insurgency campaigns. He was assigned to supervise paramilitary action teams of Montagnards in Darlac province in the Central Highlands . . .'

'Montagnards?' Dead-eye interrupted.

'Yes. Darker than the Vietnamese, the Montagnards are nomadic tribesmen who distrust their fellow South Vietnamese. But they were won over by the CIA, who directed a programme to help them defend themselves against the commies. When Petersen arrived, he was put to work with a couple of the Montagnard tribes, quickly learnt the language and eventually forged a close relationship with them. This enabled him to teach them a lot, including, apart from the standard forms of village defence, the disruption of enemy infiltration and supply routes, the destruction of enemy food crops, and various forms of raiding, ambushing and patrolling. With the subsequent help of Warrant Officer Bevan Stokes, the Montagnards were given training in weapons, demolitions, map reading and radio communications. The results were impressive, but . . .'

'Here it comes!' Jimbo put in sardonically.

'Indeed, it does . . . Petersen's work with the Montagnards gained him the honour of a tribal chieftainship, success against the VC and recognition from his superiors. But the South Vietnamese government, alarmed that in two years Petersen had developed a highly skilled Montagnard army of over a thousand men who could be turned against them in a bid for independence, brought pressure to bear, forcing him to leave the country.'

'So it's tread with care,' Dead-eye said.

Callaghan nodded. 'Yes.'

'Are the Aussies now on aggressive patrolling?' Jimbo asked.

'Yes. The watershed was in '63 and '64, when the South Vietnamese government changed hands no less than six times in eighteen months and the country descended into political chaos. Seeing what was happening, the Yanks stepped in again to rescue the situation and asked Australia for more advisers, some of whom were to operate with regular ARVN field units. This was the springboard to lifting the ban on combat. In July '64 the Australian Army Training Team was strengthened to eighty-three men and the new recruits were assigned to the 1st ARVN Division in 1 Corps. Others were posted to military commands at province and district level, where their duties included accompanying Regional Force troops on operations, taking care of hamlet security, and liaising with ARVN troops operating in their area through the US advisory teams attached to the ARVN units. Officially, this was operations advising – the first step to actual combat.'

'And now they're in combat.'

'Yes. The original members of the Team were soon followed by the 1st Battalion of the Royal Australian Regiment – nearly eight hundred men, supported by an armoured personnel carrier troop, a signals detachment and a logistics support company. Those men were established in Vietnam by June 1965, under the operational control of the US 173rd Airborne

Brigade at its HQ in Bien Hoa, north-east of Saigon, south of the Dong Nai river and the notorious VC base area known as War Zone D. Side by side with the Americans, they've been fighting the VC in that area for the past year and mopping them up. They've done a good job.'

'But we're not going there. We're going to Phuoc Tuy province,' said Dead-eye.

'Correct. Even as we talk, the first Australian conscripts are arriving there as part of the new Australian Task Force. They're based at Nui Dat and their task is to clear the VC from their base area in the Long Hai hills, known as the Minh Dam secret zone. They'll be supported by the Australian SAS and our task is to lend support to the latter.'

'They won't thank us for that,' Jimbo observed. 'Those Aussies are proud.'

'Too true,' Dead-eye said.

Callaghan tugged the cover from the blackboard behind him, raised the pointer in his hand and tapped it against the words 'PHUOC TUY', highlighted on the map with a yellow marking pen. 'The Phuoc Tuy provincial border is some fifty miles south-east of Saigon. As you can see, the province is bounded by the South China Sea, the Rung Sat swamps – a formidable obstacle to any advance – and Long Kanh and Binh Tuy provinces. The population of slightly over 100,000 is concentrated in the south central area and in towns, villages and hamlets close to the provincial capital, Baria. That area is rich in paddy-fields and market gardens. But the rest of the province, about three-quarters of it, is mostly flat, jungle-covered country, except for three large groups of mountains: the May Tao group in the north-east, the Long Hai on the southern coast, and the Dinh to the west. All these mountainous areas are VC strongholds.'

'Where's the Task Force located?' Dead-eye asked.

'Around Nui Dat. A steep hill covered in jungle and rising nearly 200 feet above the surrounding terrain. The area's big enough for an airfield and for the Task Force to move on if the new base comes under attack.'

'Major problems?' Dead-eye asked.

'The VC village fortifications of Long Phuoc and Long Tan, south-east of the base, were destroyed in a joint American and Vietnamese operation just before the Aussies moved in. The villages were laid waste and their inhabitants resettled in others nearby. While this effectively removed the VC from those two villages, it created a great deal of bitterness among the pro-VC inhabitants who are now even more busily spreading anti-government propaganda and helping to strengthen the local VC infrastructure. Meanwhile the major VC force is operating out of a chain of base areas in the northern jungles of the province, most with extensive bunker and tunnel complexes. Altogether there are seven battalions of VC in the area and they can be reinforced at short notice. Against that, the province has only one ARVN battalion permanently based there, supplemented by several Regional Force companies and the so-called Popular Forces – the PF – which are local militia platoons raised to defend the villages as well as bridges, communications facilities and so forth. They're poorly equipped, poorly trained, and repeatedly turned over by the VC'.

'Sounds wonderful,' Jimbo murmured.

'A real fairy tale,' Callaghan replied, then shrugged and continued: 'Right now the VC have the upper hand, both militarily and psychologically. They've isolated Xuyen Mock in the east and Due Than in the north, both of which contained South Vietnamese district headquarters. They've heavily infiltrated all the other districts. They regularly cut all roads in the province and tax the loyal villagers who try to get out. Nevertheless, the area's of vital strategic importance to the US build-up, with Vung Tau earmarked to become a major port, supplying the delta, Saigon and Bien Hoa. This means that Route 15 on the western edge of Phuoc Tuy has to be kept clear as a prospective military supply route from Vung Tau to Saigon. In order to do this, the Task Force has to push the VC out of the central region of the province and provide a protective umbrella for the population there. The first step in this task is the clearing of the VC from the Nui Dat base area. This job will be given to the American 173rd Brigade, aided by the Australian 5th Battalion, which is being flown in right now. The latter will be supported by the Australian SAS and we're there to advise them.'

'Does our advisory role stretch to aggressive patrolling, boss?' Dead-eye asked slyly.

Callaghan grinned. 'Officially, we're not supposed to be there at all – officially, we don't exist – so once there, I suppose we just play it by ear and do what we have to do.'

'But if we fuck up, we get no support,' Jimbo said.

'Correct.'

'When do we fly out?'

'Tomorrow. On a normal commercial flight, wearing civilian clothing. We change into uniform when we get there.'

'Very good,' Dead-eye said.

Callaghan handed each of the two men a closed folder.

'These are your travel documents and bits and pieces of useful information. Report back here at six tomorrow morning. Before then, I'll expect you to have digested everything in these folders. Finally, may I remind you once more that our presence there might cause resentment from the

Aussie troops. In other words, you may find that the hearts and minds you're trying to win aren't those of the South Vietnamese peasants, but those of the Aussie SAS. They're notoriously proud, so tread carefully. If there are no questions I'll bid you good evening, gentlemen.'

Dead-eye and Jimbo stood up and left the briefing room, carrying their top-secret folders. When they had gone, Callaghan turned to the map behind him and studied it thoughtfully. Eventually, nodding to himself, he unpinned and folded it, then went to prepare for his flight the next day.

3

Though it was still early in the morning, the sun was up and the light was brilliant, with the Long Hai hills clearly visible from the deck of the carrier HMAS *Sydney*, where the troops were waiting for the landing-craft. Most were National Servicemen, young and inexperienced, their suntans gained from three months of recruit training in the Australian heat. As the 5th Battalion advance party, they had come alone, with only a sprinkling of Australian SAS NCOs in their midst, but they would be joined by the remainder of their battalion in a few days, then by 6th Battalion, with whom they would form the 1st Australian Task Force in Vietnam. Right now, apart from being weary after the tedious twelve-day voyage from Australia, they were tense with expectation, wondering if they could manage to get to shore without either hurting themselves getting in and out of the landing-craft or, even worse, being shot at by the enemy.

'Minh Dam secret zone,' Shagger said to Red as they stood together at the railing of the carrier. 'And there,' he continued, pointing north-west to the jungle-covered hills beyond the peninsula of Vung Tau, 'is the Rung Sat swamps. They're as bad as those swamps in Malaya, so let's hope we avoid them. We can do without that shit.'

Grinning, Red adjusted his soft cap and studied the conscript troops as they scrambled from the deck into the landing-craft, to be lowered to the sea. Hardly more than schoolboys, they were wearing jungle greens, rubber-soled canvas boots and soft jungle hats. Getting into the landing-craft was neither easy nor safe, as they had to scramble across from gates in the railing, then over the steel sides of the dangling boats. This necessitated a hair-raising few seconds in mid-air, high above the sea, while laden with a tightly packed bergen and personal weapons. These included the 7.62mm L1A1 SLR, the 5.56mm M16A1 automatic rifle with the 40mm M203 grenade launcher, the 9mm L9A1 Browning semi-automatic pistol and, for those unlucky few, the 7.62mm M60 GPMG with either a steel bipod or the even heavier tripod. Also, their webbing bulged with spare ammunition and M26 high-explosive hand-grenades. Thus burdened, they moved awkwardly and in most cases nervously from the swaying deck of the ship to the landing-craft dangling high above the water in the morning's fierce heat and dazzling light.

'Shitting their pants, most of them,' Red said as he watched the conscripts clambering into the vessel.

'It'll be diarrhoea as thin as water,' Shagger replied, leaning against the railing and spitting over the side, 'if the VC guns open up from those hills. They'll smell the stench back in Sydney.'

'I don't doubt it at all, Sarge. Still, I'm sure they'll do good when the time comes to kick ass for the Yanks. All the way with LBJ, eh?'

'I wouldn't trust LBJ with my grandmother's corpse,' Shagger replied. 'But if our PM says it's all the way with him, then that's where we'll go – once we get off this ship, that is.'

Shagger and Red were the only two Australian SAS men aboard HMAS *Sydney*, present to take charge of the stores and vehicles of 3 Squadron, which were being brought in on this ship. The rest of the squadron was to be flown in on one plane directly from the SAS base at Campbell Barracks, Swanbourne, once they'd completed their special training in New Guinea in a few days' time. Meanwhile Shagger had been placed temporarily in charge of this troop of regular army conscripts and was responsible for getting them from ship to shore. Once there, he and Red would split from them and go their own way.

'Whoops! Here she comes!'

The landing-craft for Shagger's men was released from the davits and lowered to deck level, where it hung in mid-air, bouncing lightly against the hull with a dull, monotonous drumming sound. When Red had opened the gate in the railing, Shagger slapped the first man on the shoulder and said, 'Over you go, lad.'

The young trooper, eighteen at the most, glanced down the dizzying depths to the sea and gulped, but then, at a second slap on the shoulder, gripped his SLR more firmly in his left hand and, with his other, reached out to take hold of the rising, falling side of the landing-craft, and pulled himself over and into it. When he had done so, the other men, relieved to see that it was possible, likewise began dropping into the swaying, creaking vessel one after the other. When everyone was in, Shagger and Red followed suit.

'Hold on to your weapons,' the sergeant told the men packed tightly together. 'This drop could be rough.'

And it was. With the chains screeching against the davits, the landing-craft was lowered in a series of swooping drops and sudden stops, jerking back up a little and swinging from side to side. The drop did not take long, though to some of the men it seemed like an eternity and they were immensely relieved when, with a deafening roaring, pounding sound, the boat plunged into the sea, drenching them in the waves that poured in over the sides. The engine roared into life, water boiled up behind it, and it moved away from the towering side of the ship, heading for shore.

'Fix bayonets!' Shagger bawled above the combined roar of the many landing-craft now in the water.

As the bayonets were clicked into place, Shagger and Red grinned at each other, fully aware that as the VC guns had not already fired, they would not be firing; and that the men would be disembarking on to the concrete loading ramp in the middle of the busy Vung Tau port area rather than into a murderous hail of VC gunfire. In fact, the reason for making the men fix bayonets was not the possibility of attack as the landing-craft went in, but to instil in them the need to take thorough precautions in all circumstances from this point on. Nevertheless, when, a few minutes later, the landing-craft had ground to a halt, the ramp was lowered, and the men marched out on to the concrete loading ramp with fixed bayonets, the American and Vietnamese dock workers burst into mocking applause and wolf whistles.

'Eyes straight ahead!' Shagger bawled. 'Keep marching, men!'

Marching up ahead, Shagger and Red led the conscript troops to the reception area of the Task Force base, which had been set up on a deserted stretch of beach on the eastern side of the Vung Tau peninsula. The Task Force consisted of two battalions with supporting arms and logistic backup, a headquarters staff, an armoured personnel carrier squadron, an artillery regiment, an SAS squadron, plus signals, engineer and supply units, totalling 4500 men – so it was scattered across a broad expanse of beach.

'Sergeant Bannerman reporting, sir,' Shagger said to the 1st Australian Logistic Support Group (1 ALSG) warrant officer in charge of new arrivals. 'Three Squadron SAS. In temporary charge of this bunch of turnip-heads and now glad to get rid of them.'

'They all look seasick,' the warrant officer observed.

'That and a touch of nerves. They're National Servicemen, after all.'

'Not tough bastards like the SAS, right?'

'You said it.'

'Now piss off back to your SAS mates, Sarge, and let me deal with this lot. I'll soon knock them into shape.'

'Good on you, sir. Now where would the supplies for 3 Squadron be?'

'I'm regular army, not SAS. I look after my own. You've only been here five minutes and you're confessing that you've already lost your supplies? With friends like you, who needs enemies?'

'Thanks for that vote of confidence, sir. I think I'll be on my way.'

'As long as you're not in *my* way, Sarge. Now take to the hills.'

'Yes, sir!' Shagger snapped, then hurried away, grinning at Red, to look for his missing supplies. In the event, they had to be separated from the general mess of what appeared to be the whole ship's cargo, which had been thrown haphazardly on to the beach, with stores scattered carelessly among the many vehicles bogged down in the sand dunes. Luckily Shagger found that the quartermaster for 1 ALSG was his old mate Sergeant Rick McCoy, and with his help the supplies were gradually piled up near the landing zone for the helicopters.

'A nice little area,' McCoy informed Shagger and Red, waving his hand to indicate the sweeping beach, now covered with armoured cars, half-tracks, tents, piles of canvas-covered wooden crates and a great number of men, many stripped to the waist as they dug trenches, raised pup tents or marched in snaking lines through the dunes, heading for the jungle-covered hills beyond the beach. 'Between these beaches and the mangrove swamps to the west you have Cap St Jacques and the port and resort city of Vung Tau. Though Vung Tau isn't actually part of Phuoc Tuy province, it's where we all go for rest and convalescence. Apparently the VC also use the town for R and C, so we'll all be nice and cosy there.'

'You're kidding!'

'No, I'm not. That place is never attacked by Charlie, so I think he uses it. How the hell would we know? One Vietnamese getting drunk or picking up a whore looks just like any other; so the place is probably filled with the VC. That thought should lend a little excitement to your next night of bliss.'

'Bloody hell!' said Red.

In fact, neither Red nor Shagger was given the opportunity to explore the dangerous delights of Vung Tau as they were moved out the following morning to take part in the establishment of an FOB, a forward operating base, some sixteen miles inland at Nui Dat. Lifted off in the grey light of dawn by an RAAF Caribou helicopter, they were flown over jungle wreathed in mist and crisscrossed with streams and rivers, then eventually set down on the flat ground of rubber plantations surrounding Nui Dat, a small but steep-sided hill just outside Baria.

The FOB was being constructed in the middle of the worst monsoon the country had experienced for years. Draped in ponchos, the men worked in relentless, torrential rain that had turned the ground into a mud-bath and filled their shelters and weapons pits with water. Not only did they work in that water – they slept and ate in it too.

To make matters worse, they were in an area still dominated by the enemy. Frequently, therefore, as they toiled in the pounding rain with thunder roaring in their ears and lightning flashing overhead, they were fired upon by VC snipers concealed in the paddy-fields or behind the trees of the rubber plantations. Though many Aussies were wounded or killed, the others kept working.

'This is bloody insane,' Shagger growled as he tried to scoop water out of his shallow scrape and found himself being covered in more mud. 'The floods of fucking Noah. I've heard that in other parts of the camp the water's so deep the fellas can only find their scrapes when they fall into them. Some place to fight a war!'

'I don't mind,' Red said. 'A bit of a change from bone-dry Aussie. A new experience, kind of. I mean, anything's better than being at home with the missus and kids. I feel as free as a bird out here.'

'We're belly down in the fucking mud,' Shagger said, 'and you feel as free as a bird! You're as mad as a hatter.'

'That some kind of bird, is it, Sarge?'

'Go stuff yourself!' said Shagger, returning to the thankless task of bailing out his scrape.

Amazingly, even in this hell, the camp was rapidly taking shape. Styled after a jungle FOB of the kind used in Malaya, it was roughly circular in shape with defensive trenches in the middle and sentry positions and hedgehogs: fortified sangars for twenty-five-pound guns and a nest of 7.62mm GPMGs. This circular base was surrounded by a perimeter of barbed wire and claymore mines. Shagger and Red knew the mines were in place because at least once a day one of them would explode, tripped by the VC probing the perimeter defences with reconnaissance patrols. Still the Aussies kept working.

'Now I know why the Yanks fucked off,' Shagger told Red as they huddled up in their ponchos, feet and backside in the water, trying vainly to smoke cigarettes as the rain drenched them. 'They couldn't stand this bloody place. Two minutes of rain, a single sniper shot, and those bastards would take to the hills, looking for all the comforts of home and a fortified concrete bunker to hide in. A bunch of soft twats, those Yanks are.'

'They have their virtues,' Red replied. 'They just appreciate the good things in life and know how to provide them. I mean, you take our camps: they're pretty basic, right? But their camps have air-conditioners, jukeboxes and even honky-tonk bars complete with Vietnamese waiters. Those bastards are organized, all right.'

'*We've* got jukeboxes,' Shagger reminded him.

'We had to buy them off the Yanks.'

'Those bastards make money out of everything.'

'I wish *I* could', Red said.

'Well, we're not doing so badly,' said Shagger. 'This camp's coming on well.'

It was true. Already, the initial foxholes and pup tents had been replaced by an assortment of larger tents and timber huts with corrugated-iron roofs. Determined to enjoy themselves as best they could, even in the midst of this squalor, the Aussies, once having raised huts and tents for headquarters, administration, communications, first aid, accommodation, ablutions, transport, supplies, weapons and fuel, then turned others into bars, some of which boasted the jukeboxes they'd bought from the Yanks. There were also four helicopter landing zones and a single parking area for trucks, jeeps, armoured cars and tanks.

While they were waiting for the other members of 3 Squadron to arrive, Shagger and Red between them supervised the raising of a large tent to house the SAS supplies already there. The tent was erected in one day with the help of Vietnamese labourers stripped to the waist and soaked by the constant rain. When it was securely pegged down, the two SAS men used the same labourers to move in the supplies: PRC 64 and A510 radio sets, PRC 47 high-frequency radio transceivers, batteries, dehydrated ration packs, US-pattern jungle boots, mosquito nets and a variety of weapons, including SLRs, F1 Carbines and 7.62mm Armalite assault rifles with twenty-round box magazines. Shagger then inveigled 1 ALSG's warrant-officer into giving him a regular rotation of conscript guards to look after what was, in effect, 3 Squadron's SAS's quartermaster's store.

'I thought you bastards were supposed to be self-sufficient,' the warrant officer said.

'Bloody right,' Shagger replied.

'So how come you can't send enough men in advance to look after your own kit?'

'They're still mopping up in Borneo,' Shagger said, 'so they couldn't fly straight here.'

'And my name's Ned Kelly,' the warrant officer replied, then rolled his eyes and sighed. 'OK, you can have the guards.'

'I've got that prick in my pocket,' Shagger told Red when they were out of earshot of the warrant officer.

'You'll have him up your backside,' Red replied, 'if you ask for anything else.'

When construction of the camp had been completed, five days after Shagger and Red had arrived, the two men were called to a briefing in the large HQ tent. By this time the rest of 3 Squadron had arrived by plane from Perth and were crowding out the tent, which was humid after recent rain and filled with whining, buzzing flies and mosquitoes. As the men swotted the insects away, wiped sweat from their faces, and muttered a wide variety of oaths, 1 ALSG's CO filled them in on the details of the forthcoming campaign against the Viet Cong.

'The first step,' he said, 'is to dominate an area surrounding the base out to 4000 yards, putting the base beyond enemy mortar range. We will do this with aggressive patrolling. The new perimeter will be designated Line Alpha. The second step is to secure the area out to the field artillery range – a distance of about 11,000 yards. Part of this process . . .' – he paused uncomfortably before continuing – 'is the resettlement of Vietnamese living within the area.'

'You mean we torch or blow up their villages and then shift them elsewhere?' Shagger said with his customary bluntness.

The CO sighed. 'That, Sergeant, is substantially correct. I appreciate that some of you may find this kind of work rather tasteless. Unfortunately it can't be avoided.'

'Why? It seems unnecessarily brutal – and not exactly designed to win hearts and minds.'

The CO smiled bleakly, not being fond of the SAS's reputation for straight talking and the so-called 'Chinese parliament', an informal talk between officers, NCOs and other ranks in which all opinions were given equal consideration. 'The advantage of resettling the villagers is that whereas the VC aren't averse to using villagers as human shields, we can, in the event of an attack, deploy our considerable fire-power without endangering them – another way of winning their hearts and minds.'

'Good thinking,' Shagger admitted.

'I'm pleased that you're pleased,' the CO said, wishing the outspoken SAS sergeant would sink into the muddy earth and disappear, but unable to show his disapproval for fear that his own men would think him a fool. 'So one of our first tasks will be to finish the destruction of a previously fortified village located approximately a mile and a quarter south-east of this base. Huts and other buildings will be torched or blown up and crops destroyed. This we will do over a period of days. Unpleasant though this may seem to you, it's part of the vitally necessary process of reopening the province's north-south military supply route, and eventually driving the enemy back until they're isolated in their jungle bases.'

'So what's the SAS's role in all this?' Shagger asked him.

'Your task is to pass on the skills you picked up in Borneo to the ARVN troops and to engage in jungle bashing – patrolling after the VC who've turned this camp into their private firing range. Eventually, when Line Alpha has been pushed back to beyond the limits of field artillery, you'll be given the task of clearing out a VC stronghold in a bunker-and-tunnel complex. The location will be given to you when the time comes.'

'Why not give us the location now?' Red asked.

'Because the less you know the better,' the CO replied.

'You mean if we're captured by Charlie, we'll be tortured for information,' Red replied.

'Yes. And Charlie's good at that. Now, there's another important aspect to this operation. You'll be advised and assisted – though I should stress that the collaboration should be mutually beneficial – by a three-man team from Britain's 22 SAS. They'll be arriving from the old country in four days' time.'

45

A murmur of resentment filled the room and was only ended when Shagger asked bluntly: 'Why do we need advice from a bunch of Pommie SAS? We know as much about this business as they do. We can do it alone.'

'I'm inclined to agree, Sergeant, but the general feeling at HQ is that the British SAS, with their extensive experience in jungle warfare, counter-insurgency patrolling, and hearts-and-minds campaigning in places as different and as far apart as Malaya, Oman, Borneo and, more recently, Aden, have a distinct advantage when it comes to operations of this kind. So, whether you like it or not, those three men – a lieutenant-colonel and two sergeants – will soon be flying in to act as our advisers.'

'Bloody hell!' Red exclaimed in disgust.

The CO ignored the outburst. 'Are there any questions?' he asked.

As the men had none, the meeting broke up and they all hurried out of the humid tent, into the drying, steaming mud of the compound of the completed, now busy, FOB. The sky above the camp was filled with American Chinook helicopters and B52 bombers, all heading inland, towards the Long Hai hills.

4

When the USAF Huey descended over Nui Dat, having flown in from Saigon, Lieutenant-Colonel Callaghan, Jimbo and Dead-eye looked down at an FOB of the kind they had themselves constructed in Malaya: a roughly circular camp with defensive trenches in the middle and sentry positions and 'hedgehogs' – fortified sangars for twenty-five-pounders and a nest of 7.62mm GPMGs – located at regular intervals around the perimeter. This well-defended base was surrounded by another perimeter of barbed wire and – they assumed from the levelling of the ground – claymores. Surprisingly, instead of the foxholes and pup tents they had expected, they found large tents and timber huts with roofs of corrugated iron, plus four helicopter landing zones and a parking area for all the camp's vehicles.

'They've been busy,' Callaghan shouted over the roar of the helicopter. 'They only arrived here a few weeks ago. That's some job they've done.'

'Aussies work hard and play hard,' Jimbo said.

'Hard bastards,' Dead-eye said. 'You can't deny that.'

'Well, let's hope we can win their respect,' Callaghan replied.

'Good as done,' Jimbo assured him, while Dead-eye simply nodded.

As the Huey came down on one of the four LZs, its spinning rotors whipped up a cloud of dust and fine gravel that obscured the soldiers on the ground. Callaghan and his two men were out of the chopper even before the rotors had stopped spinning, stooped over and covering their eyes with their hands as they hurried out of the swirling dust. As they were straightening up again, a man wearing jungle greens with sergeant's stripes and a 9mm Browning holstered at his waist climbed down from his jeep and saluted Callaghan.

'Lieutenant-Colonel Callaghan?'

'Correct,' Callaghan replied, returning the salute. 'Two-two SAS.'

'Sergeant Bannerman, sir. Three Squadron SAS. I've been sent by the CO to collect you. Welcome to Nui Dat.'

'Thank you, Sergeant. This is Sergeant Ashman, commonly known as Jimbo, and Sergeant Parker, known to one and all as Dead-eye.'

Shagger nodded at both men, grinning slightly as he studied Dead-eye.

'I take it your nickname means you're pretty good with that SLR.'

Dead-eye nodded, and Jimbo said, 'That and everything else, mate. If it fires, Dead-eye's your man.'

'What about you, Sarge?'

'I get by,' Jimbo said.

Shagger grinned. 'Let's hope so.' He then nodded at Lieutenant-Colonel Callaghan and said, 'Right, boss, let's get to it. If you'd like to take a seat in the jeep I'll drive you straight to the boss. When you've had a chat with him, I'll show you to your quarters. By the way, they call me Shagger.'

They all laughed and piled into the jeep. The Australian drove them a short distance to a large wooden hut with a corrugated-iron roof and a sign at the top of the steps of the raised veranda, saying: 'Headquarters 3 Squadron SAS'. A second sign at the opposite side of the steps said: 'Abandon hope all ye who enter here.'

Grinning at each other, Callaghan, Jimbo and Dead-eye followed Shagger into the building. Inside was a spacious administration area sealed off behind a counter and ventilated by slowly spinning ceiling fans. Seated behind the desks were a mixture of 3 Squadron SAS and 5th Battalion male clerks, all of them looking busy. A proliferation of propaganda leaflets from the VC had been pinned to the notice-boards to entertain those waiting for their appointments, among them: 'Aussie go home: there is no resentment between the Vietnamese and the Australian people!' and 'Australian and New Zealand Armymen: Do not become Washington's mercenaries; urge your government to send you back home.'

'Someone obviously has a sense of irony,' Callaghan said.

'The VC drop them all the time,' Shagger told him. 'A wide variety. Troopers coming in here for appointments are generally amused by them. That's the favourite.' He pointed to an illustration of a handsome Australian soldier sharing drinks with a sexy lady. The caption said: 'The sensible man is home with his woman, or someone else will be. Is this war worth it?' 'Given the amount of Dear John letters that come from back home, that one's definitely ironic. This way, please.'

Shagger then led them to an office at the end of a short corridor. A sign on the open door said: 'Commanding Officer' but no name was given. They could see the CO at his desk, studying maps and charts, and when the sergeant coughed into his fist he looked up.

'Your visitors, boss,' Shagger said, ushering the three men from 22 SAS into the office. He introduced them to Lieutenant-Colonel Rex Durnford, who was blue-eyed, red-haired, suntanned and looked a lot younger than his thirty-nine years. Tipping his chair back and stretching his legs, the CO waved a hand at the scattering of chairs in front of the desk and said, 'Please be seated, gentlemen.'

Durnford smiled brightly and said, 'Well, gentlemen, far be it from me to make you feel unwelcome – and I appreciate that you're only doing your jobs – but I *do* think I'm going to have trouble explaining to my men why they should need to be advised by the British SAS.'

'We're not so much advisers as observers,' Callaghan replied. 'It's therefore felt that the advice could flow both ways.'

'Not sure what you mean by that.'

'One of the reasons we've been sent here is that we have particularly good knowledge of counter-insurgency operations and jungle survival in particular.'

'We were in Malaya as well.'

'Not like us, as I'm sure you know.'

'Nothing you did that we didn't do,' Shagger put in, though with no trace of anger – more like a man just setting the record straight.

'Granted,' Callaghan said. 'But you didn't do it as much. Nor did you do it in such a wide variety of locations. The war here isn't like the war in Malaya. It's not like Borneo either. It's like a little bit of both – the VC live a nomadic life and know the jungle well – but apart from that it's not the same thing. Therefore certain of your superiors in Canberra believe that no matter what your experiences in Malaya and Borneo, you can learn a lot from what we picked up, not only there, but also in places like Oman and the Yemen.'

'I dispute that,' Shagger said.

'You do. Canberra doesn't. And the orders to send us three here came all the way to Hereford from Canberra.'

'You're asking us to take advice regarding a war we're already involved in,' countered Shagger. 'You haven't been involved. You don't know what goes on here. With all due respect, sir, it's us who should be advising you. That's the root of the hard feelings.'

Callaghan smiled. He was pleased to note that although the Australian SAS were not related to the British, they certainly appeared to have adopted at least one of the lessons of Hereford. Sergeant Bannerman, whether he knew about Chinese parliaments or not, obviously felt at ease speaking his mind in front of his CO. Callaghan liked him for that and knew, from the expression on their faces, that Jimbo and Dead-eye felt the same.

'I understand the reason for resentment,' Callaghan said, 'but I think we can iron it out, Sergeant. As I said, this will be a two-way affair – a trade-off – and when your men see that, I believe their misgivings will fade away. We're here to offer advice in general small-team patrolling and other aspects of counter-insurgency warfare – at least as it relates to the particular way in which the VC fight. But I must repeat that we're also here to learn as much as we can from you.'

'So what can we teach you?' Lieutenant-Colonel Durnford asked.

Callaghan spread his hands in the air and said, 'We haven't been to Vietnam. We three are the first and possibly the last from 22 SAS to come here. We haven't fought people like the VC and we want to know how they think. This is a new kind of war, fought by men who can survive for extraordinary lengths of time without food, know the land intimately, are totally obedient, have little to lose, and can live for months, even years, underground. They're fighting a war of attrition, defeating vastly superior arms, particularly US air power, and we want to know what makes them tick. We also want to learn the lessons of engagement, particularly with regard to the tunnel complexes. We've never fought in such circumstances before; we want to learn what we can from it.'

'The tunnel complexes are a nightmare,' Durnford informed him. 'The men who go down into them in pursuit of the VC have the most dangerous job in Vietnam. We call them tunnel rats, and they're a very rare breed.'

'We still want that experience.'

'May I ask why you men in particular were picked for this task?'

'I was chosen because of my long-term experience with the Regiment, commencing with the LRDG in North Africa and including Malaya, Borneo and the Yemen. For the past year or so, I've been with Planning and Intelligence, in Hereford, and the information I pick up from this experience here in Vietnam will be used for future training and planning programmes. As for Sergeants Ashman and Parker, they have similar experience, though they were finally picked because of their exceptional proficiency at the double-tap – firing at close range with the Browning High Power – which we feel will come in handy when they go down into the tunnel complex.'

'Which particular complex?' Durnford asked. 'Do you have one in mind?'

'According to our intelligence, there's one located approximately five miles east of here, under a VC-held village. One of our purposes in coming here is to take part in the closing down of that complex when you secure the area out to the field artillery range.'

'I'd think twice about that if I were you,' Shagger said. 'Going down into those tunnels is a very specialized task. We may be new to this game, but we know more about it than you.'

'Good,' Jimbo said with a wicked grin. 'Then we'll go down with you.'

Shagger returned the grin, but his gaze was mocking.

'You must be scrub-happy if you think I'm going to take you down there. When I go down, I go down with my mate and no one else, thanks. I want no distractions.'

'What's scrub-happy mean?' Dead-eye asked.

'Mentally disturbed,' said Shagger.

'You have to be that way to apply for the SAS in the first place,' Jimbo informed him.

They all laughed, but the tone became serious again when Dead-eye asked, 'What's the problem? I mean, we're not exactly novices. We can react as quickly as anyone alive, so we could be useful to you and your mate, rather than distract you.'

'It's the knowledge,' Shagger said, concealing the fact, with his CO's prior agreement, that his experience of the tunnels was theoretical. For although his mate Red Swanson was a seasoned tunnel rat, he himself had never taken part in an operation to flush out VC guerrillas from an underground complex. The fact was that there were now so few survivors possessing those skills that first-rate soldiers like Shagger were having to undergo a crash training programme. 'You can't learn that until you go down. Those tunnel complexes are labyrinthine, filled with trapdoors and booby-traps. You're going into a maze – a vertical maze. It's dark, suffocating and absolutely unpredictable, with false tunnels that lead to dead-ends. As the tunnels are too narrow to turn around in, you have to get back out by crawling backwards on your hands and knees, which can cop you a VC bullet up the arsehole. Also, either VC assassins or booby-traps are waiting for you around the many sharp bends. No, to be a tunnel rat you need more experience than you can hope to learn on a single patrol.' Aware of his own complete lack of practical experience, Shagger decided to say no more.

'We're as quick with our eyes as we are with our nine-millies,' Dead-eye told him. 'We can learn what we need to know with one patrol and then do what's required.'

'I doubt that,' Shagger said.

'What Sergeant Bannerman's trying to tell you,' Lieutenant-Colonel Durnford put in, 'is that the only men presently acting as tunnel rats are the few survivors of the first forays down into the tunnels. Most men, when they go down without experience, don't came back up again. Only about twenty per cent have survived so far. That's how dangerous it is down there.'

'We've faced worse odds,' Jimbo told him.

'That's right,' Callaghan said, turning to Durnford. 'I say these men can go down with your men and come back up again. If they could survive the Keeni Meeni operations in the crowded souks and bazaars of Aden, they can survive anything thrown at them in the tunnels. It's imperative that they have this experience and I know they can cope with it.'

Lieutenant-Colonel Durnford glanced at Shagger, who shrugged, then nodded his consent and said, 'Fair enough. When the time comes you can tackle the tunnel complex with me and my mate, Red Swanson. But it's not going to happen right away.'

'Because you have to clear this area first,' Callaghan said, 'and protect the camp.'

'Exactly.'

'So what are your first objectives?'

'The first,' Lieutenant-Colonel Durnford said, 'is to go on a bit of bush-bashing to route the VC snipers and reconnaissance patrols. Though they occasionally trip claymores and blow themselves to hell, they're still managing to kill too many of our men and hamper the proper running of the base. We have to go out there in small patrols and root them out of the area, gradually pushing back the perimeter.'

'And the second?'

'To finish the destruction of a previously fortified village a mile and a quarter south-east of the base. Huts and buildings will have to be torched and blown up – and crops destroyed.'

'We can certainly help you there,' Callaghan told him. 'We'll deploy your men in four-man patrols and map out a strategy for covering the whole of the perimeter in criss-crossing elimination paths. As we clear Charlie out, we'll replace him with defensive gun emplacements, each manned by three troopers. By the time we finish, you'll have no problems with VC snipers or reconnaissance patrols.'

'Can you push that area out to at least 4000 yards?'

'Beyond mortar range?'

'Correct.'

'Yes, we can.'

'Good. That new perimeter will be designated Line Alpha. The second step, once you've completed the first, will be to secure the area out to the field artillery range. Once you've done so, we can finish off that village, which will leave us in total control of the area surrounding the base out to beyond Charlie's artillery range. Come back to me after you've accomplished that and we'll discuss the tunnels.'

Callaghan and Jimbo exchanged grins, but Dead-eye remained stony-faced. Returning his attention to Durnford, Callaghan asked, 'Anything special to look out for?'

'Yes,' Shagger said before the CO could reply. 'Booby-traps. Lots of them. All deadly. That's what you watch out for.'

'We had lots of those in Borneo and Malaya. Are they similar here?'

'Bloody right! But they're even more diabolical.'

'In what way?'

Shagger walked over to the wall at one side of the CO's desk. There he pulled down a chart to reveal a variety of drawings of different VC booby-traps, most involving punji pits, spikes, arrows, nails or bullets.

'The cartridge trap,' he said, pointing to the first of the illustrations. 'A piece of bamboo is buried in the ground with the open end exposed. The other end rests on a solid wooden board with a nail hammered through it, the sharp end facing upwards. A bullet is set into the bamboo with the flat end resting on the sharp end of the nail and the tip sticking up out of the open end of the bamboo tube. This is then hidden in soil and grass or leaves. When a soldier steps on the upper end of the cartridge, he forces it down on the nail which then acts like a firing pin, sending the bullet through the man's foot and mangling it. In fact, the bullet sometimes goes right through the foot and ends up burying itself in the man's face, which can happen if he is bending forward at the time. Not a nice way to go.'

Bannerman pointed to another drawing and said, 'This one's known as the angled arrow trap. A length of bamboo about three feet long is fastened to a piece of solid wood. Inside the bamboo, a steel arrow is held ready to fire by means of a strong rubber band and a catch machanism fixed to a trip-wire. The whole contraption is then placed in a camouflaged pit and sloped at the angle required to send the arrow through the chest of an average-sized man when he trips the wire. Naturally, if he's smaller than that, he gets it through the throat or face; if taller, through the belly or balls.'

'Ouch!' groaned Jimbo.

Shagger grinned as he pointed to a third drawing. 'The whip,' he said. 'A strong piece of green bamboo with spikes as sharp as daggers attached to it. One end of the bamboo is tied to a tree trunk, the other end to another tree trunk or fixed post so as to bend the bamboo sharply backwards. This end is held by a catch in the firing position. The catch is released by a trip-wire that makes the pole spring round and propel the spikes into the body of the victim. The spikes are usually driven in so deep that the victim dies standing upright and is held in that position by the spikes. Not a pretty sight.'

'Welcome to Vietnam,' Jimbo whispered to Dead-eye. 'Land of smiling people and fun and games.'

'Of course, you're bound to know from Malaya about the various forms of punji pits. Here, they're pretty much the same, except the pits are sometimes filled with upward-pointing steel spikes, as well as sharpened bamboo sticks, and the bamboo lid pivots on an axle to tip the man in, rather than just caving in as they usually do in Malaya and Borneo. Otherwise they're just as deadly. Another common booby-trap is the min anti-personnel mine – that's m-i-n, not mini – which looks like a German stick grenade with a short handle. This handle contains a pull-friction delay fuse that's operated by a trip-wire hidden by foliage or grass and usually laid across a jungle path. So you have to watch what you step on at all times, which makes for pretty slow going through the bush. Then there are the usual natural dangers, such as wild boar, pig, poisonous snakes, stinging hornets, mosquitoes . . .'

'Right,' Jimbo said. 'I think we've got the picture, Sergeant.'

'Good,' Durnford said. 'Any more questions, gentlemen?'

When Callaghan glanced at Jimbo and Dead-eye, they both shook their heads. 'No questions,' Callaghan replied, 'except, where do we basha down?'

'Pardon?'

'Bunk up,' Dead-eye clarified.

'You got here just in time,' the CO replied. 'We've just moved out of trenches and pup tents into wooden barracks. You, Lieutenant-Colonel, will be in the officers' barracks with me and the other officers. You two men will be in the NCOs' barracks. Sergeant Bannerman will show you to your quarters. Have a good night's rest, gentlemen. You'll be moving out tomorrow.'

Shagger led them out of the building and across the central clearing of the camp, which included a flattened area used as a football pitch. Helicopters were taking off, aircraft rumbling overhead, troop trucks entering and leaving, twenty-five-pounders in hedgehogs firing the odd shell purely for the purposes of harassment, the GPMG gunners firing test bursts, and other troopers bawling at one another as they worked at various tasks. The new arrivals found their ceaseless activity familiar and reassuring.

They separated – Callaghan to enter the officers' barracks, Jimbo and Dead-eye the building beside it – and unpacked what kit they wouldn't need on their assignment. When they were ready, Jimbo and Dead-eye left and crossed to the mess tent with Shagger for a good nosh-up, washed down with beer. There they met Shagger's mate Corporal Red Swanson, the tunnel rat.

5

'Sergeants Ashman and Parker, from 22 SAS, Hereford, England,' Shagger said, indicating the two visitors with the pork sausage pronged by the fork he was holding as Red, carrying a plate and eating utensils, plopped down on the bench seat beside him. 'Jimbo and Dead-eye to you.'

They were in the large mess tent, which was filled with soldiers from the 5th and 6th Battalions of the 1st Australian Task Force in Vietnam, 1 and 3 Squadrons of the Australian Special Air Service (SAS), the 17th Construction Squadron, and a few members of the South Vietnamese Civil Guard and the regular ARVN reaction forces. Many of the men were stripped to the waist and pouring sweat; others were in uniform. Still others were wearing a bizarre mixture of civilian clothes, notably T-shirts emblazoned with cartoon figures and rude messages, baggy shorts, sandals and a wide variety of jungle hats. A lot of food was being eaten, washed down with pints of cold beer, and though the tent was open at both ends, it was rapidly filling up with the smoke from the cigarettes that nearly everyone was smoking. The conversation was loud and ebullient, shredded by raucous laughter.

'This is my mate, Red – Red Swanson,' Shagger continued. 'The tunnel expert I told you about. He's a bloody good man.'

Jimbo and Dead-eye nodded at Red as he settled into his seat, swallowed a mouthful of mashed potatoes, then said, 'The blokes from England, come to give us advice. Some bloody joke, that is!'

'We haven't come just to give you advice,' Jimbo answered diplomatically. 'We've come to exchange tactics and information; to learn from each other.'

Red shoved hot sausage and peas into his mouth, chewed, swallowed, then grinned at Shagger. 'They've come to give us advice,' he repeated.

'We can all use some advice now and then,' Dead-eye said solemnly. 'It's a two-way process.'

'Not for me, it ain't. I've taken all the advice I can stand from my own bloody officers. I don't need it from a couple of Pommie NCOs who've never even fought here.'

'We've fought everywhere else,' Jimbo said firmly. 'You name it, we've been there.'

'That counts for bollocks here, mate. What counts here is experience on the ground – and *under* the ground. That's something you don't have.'

'We can learn from each other,' Dead-eye insisted. 'Give support to each other. That's the point of us being here.'

Red glanced at Shagger and said, 'What do you think?'

Shagger studied Jimbo and Dead-eye in turn, then said: 'I think they'll have to prove themselves first. But why not give them a try?'

Red shrugged. In the end he preferred to get on with people. 'OK,' he said. 'Let's see how they shape up.'

'We'll shape up,' Dead-eye assured him. 'Anything you care to throw at us, we'll bounce it right back.'

'*We* won't be throwing anything at you,' Shagger told him. 'The VC will.'

'We can handle it,' Dead-eye said.

'Our visitors have spirit,' Shagger said. 'OK, gentlemen,' he added, raising his glass of beer. 'Let's have a truce for now.'

'I'll second that,' Jimbo said.

The four men raised and touched their beer glasses, then quenched their relentless thirst.

'Let me buy a round,' Jimbo said.

'Sure,' said Shagger, knowing exactly what Jimbo was doing and deciding to profit by it.

Jimbo went off to the bar and returned with four pint glasses balanced expertly between his hands. When he'd distributed the beers and they'd all had another drink, Dead-eye, always keen on military facts, said: 'I'm a little bit vague on how you blokes ended up here. Do you mind filling me in?'

'We first came in 1962,' Shagger replied.

'I believe it began with a crash training programme,' Dead-eye said.

'Bloody oath,' Red replied. 'With the Team – the Australian Army Training Team Vietnam. First, a two-week briefing on the war at the Intelligence Centre in Sydney; then an intensive five days at the Canungra Jungle Training Centre in Queensland.'

'What kind of training?'

'Jungle navigation, ambushing, patrolling and sharpshooting, finishing off with sneaker and shooting galleries.'

'What?'

Red sighed at the Pom's ignorance. 'We use a demonstration platoon to teach trainees the functions they'll have to perform in the field. Each man wears a coloured helmet identifying his role in the platoon, and trainees watch the actions of individuals as the group goes through field formations or ambush drills. What we call sneaker and shooting gallery exercises teach you to react instantly to enemy targets in the jungle or at night. It's a bit like your "Killing House" in Hereford, only outdoors.'

'How does it work?' Jimbo asked.

'Each man is ordered to sneak silently through a patch of pretend enemy-held jungle. As he does this, concealed targets in the shape of enemy soldiers suddenly pop up one after the other – in your face, to one side, sometimes to the rear. You only have a split second to blast the target with your weapon or be declared a casualty. Bloody good training.'

'What happened after that?' Dead-eye asked.

'We were flown in civvies on a regular commercial flight from Singapore to Saigon,' Shagger told him. 'That was in August '62. There were twenty-nine of us. When we arrived at Tan Son Nhut airport we were met by the Australian ambassador and senior Allied officers, given a golden hand-shake, then sent out to have a good time in Saigon – a last supper, so to speak.'

'It must've been some town then,' Jimbo said with genuine envy.

'Bloody oath!' Red exclaimed, taking up the story. 'I mean, the whole bloody war was going on just a few miles away, but you wouldn't have known it when you were in Saigon . . .'

'Biggest damn city in Vietnam,' Shagger cut in. 'Capital of South Vietnam, over a million people, primary objective of the communists, but in '62 you'd have thought you were in some French colonial paradise. Downtown you had hordes of bicycles, rickshaws, Honda scooters and Renault taxis – all doing terrific business – and a little farther out you had lush tropical gardens, tree-lined boulevards and the mansions of the rich. A beaut of a city.'

'Not now, though,' Red said. 'It was changing even when we were there. No sooner had we arrived – but particularly after the Yanks arrived – than the opportunists, crooks and pimps started opening cheap bars and seedy clubs between the old restaurants and pavement cafés. Suddenly those beautiful little Vietnamese dolls in black trousers, white *ao dais* and straw hats were replaced by a horde of tit-flashing whores – them and their pimps – and God knows how many pickpockets and con men. And there were plenty of beggars too. Then the clean atmosphere was fouled up by military vehicles, and what was a relatively peaceful place became a nightmare, with the constant noise of trucks, helicopters, aircraft, exploding VC mortar shells, and music and bawling from clubs. Almost overnight it turned into a real piss-hole.'

'It's still bloody exciting, though,' Shagger said quickly, lest they get the wrong impression.

'Too right,' Red agreed. 'Best place for R and C you can imagine, despite it all.'

'And after Saigon?' Dead-eye asked.

'We were split into two separate units,' Shagger told him. 'The first unit – ten of us – was sent to the Vietnamese National Training Centre at Dong Da, south of Hue. That camp was responsible for the training of recruits for the ARVN, but the base was also used as a battalion training centre and could accommodate about a thousand men. It was a bloody tip-heap. Our living quarters, the general hygiene, rations, even the training itself, were all bloody awful. We lived in long fibro huts that had no windows, just window spaces to let the breeze in. But they also let in the rain and, even worse, bloodthirsty mosquitoes and hornets. As for the open bogs and kitchens, they were filthy, swarming with rats and every imaginable kind of creepy-crawly.

Practically all the ARVN officers were corrupt as buggery, including the commandant, and they pocketed most of the loot intended to feed us and the ARVN guys. Those same officers were crap as leaders. They'd been chosen for their social position rather than their abilities, and promoted because of their brown-nosing to those higher up, not because of their success at what they were doing. Because of this, discipline – and morale – were at rock bottom and most Vietnamese units were no more than uniformed rabble. Bloody savages, I tell you, mate!'

'And now, after the ARVN and the South Vietnamese, you think you're going to get fucked up by us,' Jimbo suggested boldly.

Shagger stared steadily, thoughtfully at him, then said, 'This is my second trip to 'Nam, and now I'm told I'm going to get advice on fighting here, courtesy of the revered SAS of Great Britain. How would *you* feel?'

'Pretty fucking miffed,' Jimbo admitted. 'But believe me, we're not here to tell you what to do. Only to work alongside you, and maybe you'll benefit from our even broader experience, picked up in a lot of different countries over the past twenty-odd years. After all, no matter how good you boys are, the Australian SAS was only formed in 1957, which means you've had less experience than us.'

Shagger wasn't about to take this lying down. 'Just like you,' he said, 'we fought in Malaya and Borneo. We've got the experience, mate.'

'But we've fought in North Africa, Sicily, Italy and all over Europe in World War II,' Jimbo insisted, 'plus South Arabia, Aden and the Yemen. That gives us an awful lot more experience of different combat techniques. In fact, it was us who created hearts-and-minds, which you're using here to win over the South Vietnamese peasants. So, you know, you can learn from us.'

'We can't learn about Vietnam from you,' Red insisted. 'You'll have to learn that from *us*.'

'We're always keen to learn,' Dead-eye told him. 'So let's not work against each other, but *with* each other. Together we'll form an even stronger team. Nothing wrong with that, is there?'

Shagger glanced at Red, grinned slightly, then turned back to Dead-eye. 'You guys have a hell of a reputation, but I still have my doubts,' he said. 'Let's wait and see how you get on when we go on our bush-bash tomorrow. You'll get a fair crack of the whip and we'll see if you're as good as you're supposed to be. If you are, we'll play ball. If you're not, it'll have been a wasted journey for you, because you'll be going nowhere with us again. Fair enough?'

Dead-eye nodded his agreement.

'Fair enough,' Jimbo said. He polished off his beer, glanced down at his empty plate, then had a good look around the mess tent. Eating and drinking with gusto, the men were shouting to make themselves heard above the loud-speakers suspended from the canvas roof and blaring out Frank Sinatra's latest hit, 'Strangers in the Night'. 'It's like a fucking nightclub,' he said.

'Well, apart from the open-air movies,' Shagger replied, 'it's one of the only two places to go and relax – either here or the bar. Which is where me and Red are going right now. Fancy a beer?'

'I think we'll give it a miss,' Dead-eye said, after catching the look in Jimbo's eye. 'It's been a long flight out and we've got to finish sorting out our kit for our first taste of bush-bashing with you guys tomorrow. And I wouldn't mind catching up on some sleep.'

Shagger pulled a face at Red. 'These Pommies must be a bit on the soft side. What do you think?'

'I'm bound to agree, Shagger. What cobber worth his salt would want to sleep when he could have a good piss-up? They must be as soft as a baby's bum.'

Jimbo grinned as he and the stony-faced Dead-eye, refusing to rise to the bait, pushed back their chairs and climbed to their feet. 'We'll see about that tomorrow,' he said, 'when we're out in the bush. For now, no matter what you hard men say, we're going to sort out our kit and get some shut-eye. We'll see you at first light.'

'We'll be ready and waiting,' Shagger said, 'with or without sleep.'

Jimbo nodded at Dead-eye and they left the mess tent, stepping into the faded light of the evening to see the palm trees sinking into silhouette against a rich, pink-hued sky. Walking side by side across the compound to their barracks, they passed the bar tent, where they heard drunken laughter, bawling and the sounds of the Walker Brothers. Glancing in, they saw a lot of red, sweaty faces illuminated in a gloom eerily coloured by the flickering lights of a Wurlitzer jukebox.

Tempted, they glanced at each other, but the puritanical Dead-eye shook his head, determined to be in tiptop condition the next morning. They walked on, passing the motor pool, which contained, in addition to jeeps and Bedford trucks, M113A1 armoured personnel carriers and fifty-ton Centurion Mark V tanks, each armed with an 83mm twenty-pound gun, a .50-calibre Browning machine-gun, and two .30-calibre Browning machine-guns. Each tank also had a 455-litre auxiliary fuel tank on its rear plate and infrared night-vision equipment.

'Very tasty,' Jimbo said.

As they neared the barracks, two Huey helicopters were coming in for the night, descending vertically and noisily through the billowing clouds of dust sucked up by their rotors. West of the landing zones, troopers dressed in jungle greens, with soft caps on their heads and their faces blackened with stick camouflage, entered the camp along the camouflaged patrol route entry, which enabled them to pass safely through the many claymores buried around the perimeter. They were armed with 7.62mm L1A1 SLRs, 5.56mm M16A1 gas-operated automatic rifles with M203 grenade launchers, 7.62mm Armalite assault rifles and M60 GPMGs. Some were carrying wounded men on stretchers; all looked extremely weary.

'Looks like they've had a hard day,' Jimbo said.

'Our turn tomorrow,' Dead-eye reminded him.

In the barracks, they found all the camp-beds empty and deduced that the Aussies, like Shagger and Red, were at the open-air movie or in the mess tent or pub. This gave them the first privacy they'd had since arriving, and they were grateful. Later, when they had sorted out their kit, they rested fully clothed on their beds, under their mosquito nets.

Propped up against his pillow, Dead-eye was studying maps of the terrain. Jimbo was stretched out on his back with his hands clasped behind his head, his gaze mesmerized by the fan spinning slowly above him.

'So what do you think of our Aussie friends, then?' he asked Dead-eye.

'Hard men. Know what they're doing. They're going to test us pretty rigorously and we'll have to match up to them.'

'I've never really thought about the Aussie SAS before. I mean, are they related to 22 Squadron?'

'No. They've nothing to do with the British regiment.' Dead-eye's hobby was reading military histories and he knew all about the Australian SAS. 'They came into being after their government agreed to send an infantry battalion to Malaya during the Emergency. That was in 1955, though it actually evolved out of the airborne platoon of the Royal Australian Regiment, which was formed in October 1951 and detached to the School of Land/Air Warfare at RAAF base Williamtown. By 1953 that platoon had become a separate unit on the army order of battle and began to take on an élite aspect, like us. In 1956, when Australia and New Zealand were asked to help with the Emergency, the Kiwis raised their own SAS squadron solely for service in Malaya and the Aussies raised a regular brigade group, 1 Australian Infantry Brigade. This consisted of two infantry battalions, one armoured regiment, a field artillery regiment, a field engineer squadron, and a special air service squadron.'

'Bob's your uncle!' Jimbo exclaimed.

'The Special Air Service squadron was a completely new unit whose members were culled mainly from the existing airborne platoon based at Williamtown. Now 1 Australian Infantry Brigade was located at Holsworthy, near Sydney, but as the emphasis with the Special Air Service squadron was naturally on air services, it was allotted to the Royal Australian Regiment as the 1st Special Air Service Company. It was located at Campbell Barracks, Swanbourne, near Perth, which is where it remains to this day.'

'So they've nothing to do with us at all.'

'No.'

'I noticed they wear a red beret, like our commandos.'

'Yes, because they're primarily an infantry-commando unit. Originally their beret badge was the crossed rifles of the Royal Australian Infantry Corps, but in 1960, when the regiment became a unit of the Royal Australian Regiment, its beret badge was changed from Infantry Corps to that of the RAR. About two years later, the link between the 1st SAS Company and the RAR was broken and it became the Special Air Service Regiment. It was then expanded to provide a base squadron and four SAS squadrons. Though not connected to our SAS, in 1965 the Aussie SAS was invited to help us out in Malaya, which they did, before joining us in Borneo. Though they're an infantry-commando-style unit, rather than an air service squadron, their roles and tactics are similar to ours, including reconnaissance through winning hearts and minds. That may be why they resent us. They probably think we look on them as pupils, rather than equals. That's bound to rankle.'

'They'll get over it,' Jimbo said.

At that moment they were both distracted by a deep, throbbing sound that had approached from the west and was now growing louder directly above the barracks. Rolling off their beds, they went to the window and glanced up at the night sky. Flying directly overhead, silhouetted by a star-bright sky, were about twenty US B52 bombers, heading inland to attack the enemy positions on the Long Hai hills. Even as Jimbo and Dead-eye looked up, amazed by the sheer number of aircraft, they heard a distant pounding coming from the east side of the barracks, directly behind them. They turned away from the window and hurried to the other side to look out of the windows.

The B52s' bombardment had already begun and great balls of silvery-yellow and orange flames were rolling along the dark mass of hills to the east, obliterating the stars with a boiling black smoke that was illuminated from within by more darting fingers of flame, like millions of fireflies. The bombing raid went on and on, filling the air with distant thunder, turning the dark hills into an eerie, dreadful vision of rolling, spewing flames and boiling black smoke that eventually appeared to cover them completely, as if obliterating everything contained there with its awesome destructive power.

'That's our calling-card,' Dead-eye said. 'We're on our way, Jimbo.'

6

Lieutenant-Colonel Callaghan was understandably nervous the following morning when, just after dawn, he addressed the men of 1 and 3 Squadrons SAS, most of whom, as he well knew, were extremely sceptical of him and his two NCOs, Jimbo and Dead-eye. For this reason the latter pair had made a point of not being beside him when he commenced his lecture.

'They'll consider it grandstanding,' Dead-eye had told him. 'So Jimbo and I should take our places with 3 Squadron, beside Shagger and Red. We'll be more anonymous that way.'

'In the audience, he means,' Jimbo said sardonically. 'The best of luck, boss.'

Now, in the briefing tent, standing on a packing crate in order to let his audience see him, Callaghan felt that he was truly on the stage, and what was more, in a very bad play. He felt this because of the cynicism he saw in that sea of faces in front of him. Before speaking, he took a deep breath and let it out slowly.

'Before proceeding with the briefing proper,' he began, 'may I just say that I understand perfectly why some of you will undoubtedly resent the fact that three members of the

British SAS have been sent here to accompany an Australian operation.'

'Hear, hear!' a voice in the crowd called out mockingly.

Callaghan nodded and smiled, acknowledging the jibe, then continued. 'Please let me emphasize, however, that we're not here to take you men over, but to exchange ideas and tactics in order to give more muscle to both regiments. We're not here to tell you what to do. We're here to take part in certain operations in order to learn from them. As for this morning's operation, please let me point out that while I'm nominally in charge of it, I'm really only here to learn and the actual planning of it was the responsibility of your own CO, Lieutenant-Colonel Durnford.'

That white lie received a smattering of applause and a few cheers. When they had died down, Callaghan said, 'So I hope that you can view me and my two men as honorary members of your Squadron, here to exchange ideas, and that you'll give us your fullest cooperation. And so to the briefing.'

He waited until the murmurs had subsided, then picked up a pointer and tapped the blackboard with it. A surprisingly detailed plan of the forward operating base had been drawn in chalk. He tapped the marked patrol route exit leading through the mined perimeter.

'The operation commencing today will be codenamed Alpha. Its purpose is to secure this FOB and then push back the perimeter to at least 4000 yards, taking it beyond enemy mortar range.' He ran the pointer around the drawn perimeter, then lowered it to his side and turned to the listening men. 'I don't have to tell you that this camp is under constant threat from VC snipers and reconnaissance patrols. Indeed, too many of your friends have been killed by them for you not to know. So our primary objective for the next few days is to clear the present perimeter of VC, place our own men in their present sniper positions, and turn their patrol routes into ambush positions. This will prevent them getting within firing range of the camp and secure those same routes for our own supply purposes.'

'About bloody time!' someone called out.

When the murmurs of approval had died down, Callaghan said, 'Well, I'm glad you agree. Your CO will be pleased.' He let the subsequent laughter expend itself before continuing. 'In order to clear the perimeter we're going to break you up into four-man patrols, each with a selected area of the perimeter to cover. As you know, the perimeter beyond our own surrounding minefield consists mainly of paddy-fields, the forests of rubber plantations and stretches of dense jungle. For this reason, we'll be supported by the UH 1B Iroquois helicopters of No. 9 Squadron RAAF, located at Vung Tau. The Iroquois will be used for troop transfers, extractions and reconnaissance. We will keep in constant contact with each other and with the choppers by means of a combination of A510 radios, PRC 64 radio sets and some USAF PRC 47 high-frequency radio transceivers. Though we'll be eyeballing the enemy on the ground, the choppers will support us with aerial reconnaissance and direct the nearest groups by radio to any enemy sighted. In the event that an individual group, or number of groups, will be required to move out of their selected patrol area to another location, the choppers will extract them and insert them at the new DZ. The choppers will also be used for casevacs and resups. As each group's patrol area is cleared of VC snipers or patrols, the enemy sniper positions and patrol routes will be taken over by our own men and the remaining men from that cleared area will be moved to another location. In this manner we can gradually cover the whole outside perimeter, push it back to a minimum of 4000 yards, designated Line Alpha, and thus secure the camp from enemy snipers, patrols, mortars and, eventually, big guns. Any questions so far?'

'You say we're being broken up into groups of four,' Shagger asked. 'We normally patrol in groups of ten. Why four-man patrols?'

'The four-man patrol is the fundamental operational unit of 22 SAS.' Grinning, Callaghan waved his free hand to silence the jeers and whistles. 'I know you don't want to hear this, but experience gained as far back as World War II has shown us that the four-man team is the most efficient and effective size for combining minimum manpower demands with maximum possibility of surprise. We've also learnt that in situations that produce great tension, the four-man team is the one most psychologically sound because the men can team up in pairs and look out for each other both domestically and tactically.'

'What do you mean by domestically?' someone called out.

'Building a hide or observation post, cooking, brewing up, washing utensils, and so forth,' Callaghan said over the wave of laughter and hooting.

'Four-man teams in bloody aprons!' someone else bawled. 'They'll soon have us in high heels!'

Callaghan patiently waited until the ribaldry had run its course before continuing. 'Each man in the four-man teams will have his specialist duty, while being able to use his cross-training for another duty, if required. Each team will therefore have a specialist in signalling, demolitions, medicine and, in case prisoners are taken, language – in this case Vietnamese. Also, for this particular operation, each four-man team will be matched to another and keep in close touch with it, ready to call in the other team, or to be called in by it, for assistance should contact be made with the enemy. In other words, in a conflict situation, the four-man team will be at least doubled in strength to turn it into an effective fighting patrol.'

'A four-man patrol doesn't allow for too much equipment, so what are we taking?' someone asked from the back of the tent.

'As I said, the four-man patrol combines minimum manpower with maximum potential for surprise. The patrol is therefore limited in its kit to what each individual can personally carry: personal weapons, bergen, hand-grenades and parts of the team's GPMG. What you lose in weapon power you gain with the possibility of surprise.'

'What about claymores or grenade launchers?'

'Neither.'

'Why not?'

'Though the individual groups will be spread all around the perimeter, they'll be in close proximity to one another, with some possibly overlapping into another's allotted patrolling area, even while being obscured from each other by rubber trees or dense forest. No weapons will therefore be fired until the enemy has been eyeballed on the ground, irrespective of locations given by the reconnaissance choppers. The resultant engagements will virtually be close-combat fire-fights, which places the enemy too close to you – and the patrols too close to each other – for the use of mines or grenade launchers. Any more questions?'

'Sir!' An Aussie raised his right hand and asked: 'So far, our patrols have been going out in the morning and returning to base at first light. Will this stay the same?'

'No. This is a long-term operation to clear the whole perimeter, push it back, and replace Charlie with our own men. For this reason you'll be required to stay out until the job is completed.'

'Full survival kit?'

'Correct. Any further questions?'

'Yeah,' said another Aussie. 'When do we move out?'

Callaghan checked his watch. 'Noon,' he said. 'As you already have your personal weapons, you can prepare fairly quickly and meet on the parade ground an hour from now. There you'll be allocated to your particular four-man team and each team given its backup team and grid references for its selected patrolling area. Stick make-up for yourselves, please, and jungle camouflage for your personal weapons. Once you're in separate teams, the teams will be sent individually to the armoury to collect a GPMG and radio and, in the case of the PC, a SARBE beacon for communication with the support-extraction choppers. You'll then gather together back at the parade ground, be marched out through the patrol route exit, and disperse to your allotted areas of patrol once outside the defensive perimeter. That's it, men. Get going.'

As the briefing broke up and the men dispersed to their barracks or tents, Callaghan indicated with his jabbing finger Jimbo, Dead-eye and the two Aussie SAS men, Shagger and Red. When these four had gathered around him, he said, 'Since you men have already met, you'll make up one team. That was my intention from the start, which is why you're in the same barracks.'

'I guessed that,' Dead-eye said.

'A little bit of bullshit is OK,' Callaghan said, 'but don't let it get out of hand when it comes to comparisons between the Brits and the Aussies. Bullshit can start as gentle banter and end up as a fist-fight. You lot have to work as two pairs of a four-man team – Dead-eye with Shagger, Jimbo with Red – and I expect you to be strongly supportive of each other, regardless of your differences of outlook. Is that understood?'

'Yes, boss,' Dead-eye said, while the other men nodded their reluctant agreement. 'I think we've all got the message.'

'Right, then, get to it.'

Following most of the others, the four men marched across the parade ground, lowering their heads and shielding their eyes from the dust that was being blown up by the two Huey helicopters ascending from the LZ. Temporarily deafened by the noise, they said nothing until they were in the barracks, by the beds grouped together at the far end.

'Nice little ear-bashing from your boss,' Red said. 'I could tell he's concerned for our welfare. Or *your* welfare, at least.'

'Doesn't want us to get into a blue over bullshit flying out of control,' Shagger added, grinning. 'As if that could happen!'

'A blue?' Jimbo asked.

'A fight,' Red informed him.

'I always thought the Aussies spoke English,' Jimbo said. 'Now I'm beginning to wonder. We're going out to have a blue on a bush-bash after having an ear-bash. They might as well be speaking fucking Swahili!'

As Red started transferring unwanted kit from his bergen to the steel locker beside his bed, he looked up and said, 'You bastards cross-grain the buckets, take orders from your head shed and the other Ruperts, attack the enemy with mixed-fruit puddings, fire double-taps from nine-millies, get intelligence from the green slime in the Kremlin, go on the piss in the Sports and Social, then get some kip in the spider. If that's English, mate, I've been speaking another language since the day I was born.'

'What did he just say?' Dead-eye asked deadpan.

'Don't know,' Jimbo replied. 'I didn't understand a fucking word. Maybe he was speaking Vietnamese. Let's make him the language specialist of our team.'

'*I'm* the language specialist,' Shagger informed him. 'And my speciality is Vietnamese, so you've no problem there.'

'It's your English that's the problem with me, mate. How about sign language?'

'The only sign I'll be giving you, cobber, is this,' said Red, giving him the two fingers.

'As long as it's purely visual,' Jimbo said, grinning broadly, 'we'll understand each other fine.'

As they were going out on a long-term mission, there wasn't much they could remove from their packed bergens and store in their lockers apart from a few personal items. Because of the demands of the patrol, the rucksacks still contained the heavier items, including survival kit, water bottle, waterproof poncho, survival bag and spare ammunition. When all of this had been packed in or strapped on, they proceeded to check and camouflage their personal weapons: 7.62mm L1A1 SLRs for Jimbo and Dead-eye, 5.56mm M16A1 automatic rifles for Shagger and Red, and Browning 9mm High Power handguns for all of them. Each man's Browning was holstered normally on his hip, but the recognizable outline of his rifle was disguised by wrapping the barrel with strips of cloth dyed to match the green and brown of the rubber trees and denser forest. The pistol grip, magazine and top cover were covered with pieces of disruptive-pattern material held on with masking tape.

'All joking aside,' Shagger said as he camouflaged his rifle, 'that Lieutenant-Colonel Callaghan seems pretty impressive to me. Not some upper-class Pommy ponce educated at Eton.'

'You're right to be impressed,' Dead-eye replied. 'Callaghan isn't upper class, he isn't a ponce and he was educated in the field rather than Eton. In fact, he's a former Irish rugby international and accomplished boxer. Originally with 3 Commando, he was in a military prison in Cairo for knocking out his CO, waiting to go on trial, when Stirling got him released to help in the formation of the first SAS squadron, way back in 1941.'

'He knocked out his CO?' Shagger asked, raising his eyebrows.

'That's right. Though Callaghan's normally good-natured and polite, he has a notorious temper. In fact, before knocking the bloke out, he ran him out of the officers' mess at the point of a bayonet.'

'I like the sound of that,' Shagger said.

'Me too,' Red agreed.

'So Stirling got him out of the cooler,' Shagger said, 'and then they started the SAS.'

Dead-eye nodded. 'Correct.'

'That was in 1941,' Jimbo said. 'I was there at the time. A twenty-year-old private. We trained at a hell-hole called Kabrit, in the Suez Canal Zone, and there was nothing that Callaghan asked us to do that he didn't do himself. Christ, he was tough! Once, after a murderous march, when one of my mates complained that we had to stop for a rest, Callaghan, who stopped for no one or nothing, grabbed the berk by the shoulders, picked him bodily off the ground, and held him over the edge of the cliff we were hiking along, threatening to drop him into the fucking sea. There were no more complaints after that.'

Shagger chuckled while Red looked on, wide-eyed.

'As for engaging with the enemy,' Jimbo continued, 'again he never asked you to do anything he wouldn't do himself.

Of course, since he was so bloody fearless, he was constantly getting us to do things that we thought were either impossible or suicidal. But we did them. Pulled them off. He set a shining example.'

'I heard about you fellas in the desert,' Shagger told him. 'You inserted by parachute in the middle of bad storms. You raided German airfields in heavily armed jeeps, attacking on the move and roaring out again before they could catch you. You hiked halfway across the bloody desert. You worked with the Long Range Desert Group. Looks like you've done it all, mate.'

'We have,' Jimbo said proudly. 'And Daddy Callaghan was on practically every mission. He was out there in front.'

'Same in Malaya,' Dead-eye said. 'He spent months all alone in the jungle, living off the land and spying on the commies. He came out of it looking like a scarecrow, fed and exercised himself back to health, then led the whole bloody squadron right back in there. That man was amazing.'

Red gave a low whistle of admiration while Shagger just shook his head from side to side and said, 'Well, let's hope you guys are as good.'

'No one's as good as Callaghan,' Dead-eye admitted, 'but we're pretty damn close to it.'

'We'll soon see,' Shagger told him.

When the weapons had been disguised, each man camouflaged himself by using 'cam' cream to cover the exposed areas of his skin – face, neck, wrists and hands. The cream was applied in three stages: first, a thin base coating diluted with saliva to cover all exposed areas; second, the painting of diagonal lines of stick camouflage across the face, to break up the shape and outline of the features; finally, darkening highlighted areas such as forehead, nose, cheek-bones and chin. Then the men donned their green bush hats, which, along with their bergens, webbing, M26 high-explosive hand-grenades, and the separate components of the team's GPMG and the radio (the latter two items still to be obtained from the armoury tent), would be camouflaged with pieces of the vegetation to be found outside the perimeter.

When all was completed, the four men took turns at checking each other to ensure that nothing had been missed.

'I knew most Pommies were pansies,' Red said as he inspected the back of Jimbo's neck and behind his ears, 'but I didn't appreciate they were so good with make-up.'

'I've heard that Aussies are so hard,' Jimbo replied, 'because they're trying to hide the fact that they're really fairies. No wonder you managed to make up so quickly; you must do it all the time.'

'Ha, ha,' Red said touchily.

'All right, you two,' Shagger warned them. 'That's enough for now. Let's just finish this mutual inspection and get back outside. We're running late as it is.'

In silence the four men hauled on their bergens, picked up their personal weapons and headed back to the parade ground, which now was baking in the late-morning heat, even though the southern sky was darkening with clouds.

'Rain,' Shagger said, sounding grim.

'Shit,' Red replied with a weary shake of his head.

The parade ground was already filling up with most of the other men from 1 and 3 Squadrons, who were milling about in front of a notice-board placed at the edge of the field. Lieutenant-Colonels Callaghan and Durnford were standing beside Sergeant-Major Art Wheeler, looking on as the men, all now heavily laden, checked where their names were in the typed lists pinned to the board. When each man found his own name within a four-man group, he called out his group number and was sent by the sergeant-major to join that group. These groups were placed next to those who would give them backup and sarcastic jokes were being bawled back and forth between them.

'With a shower like you giving us support,' Corporal Dan Allen shouted at Shagger and Red, clearly meaning to include the two Pommies, Jimbo and Dead-eye, 'it's a case of God protect us from our friends!'

'God only protects the worthy,' Shagger bawled back, 'and that leaves you lot out!'

As the most experienced men there, Jimbo, Dead-eye, Shagger and Red were in Team 1, backed up by Team 2, consisting of Sergeants Don Ingrams and Giles Norton, plus two Corporals, Bob 'Blue' Butler and Michael 'Mad Mike' Dalton, all of whom had fought in Borneo just a few months ago.

'They really know their stuff,' Red told Jimbo and Dead-eye, after identifying them, 'but we can't admit that. We like to take the piss out of them. Keep their feet on solid ground. Hey, Blue!' he bawled. 'Is it true that every time you hear a shot fired, your hair turns grey? I mean, down below too?'

'My hair only turns grey, mate, when I'm given two Pommies and bludgers like you and Shagger as backup. Even God would turn grey at the thought of *that*, so don't come it, you drongo!'

'Seems to me . . .' Red was retorting until interrupted by Sergeant-Major Wheeler, who bawled, 'Pipe down, you grog-happy poofters. *I want silence this second!*' When the men had settled down, Wheeler held a pile of maps high in the air and said, 'As I call out the team number, I want the patrol commander of that team to come up and take his numbered map. Details of the team's area of patrol are given on each map. Once every PC has his map, the patrols will go one by one to the armoury and pick up their radio SARBE beacon and GPMG. I know you're just a bunch of bloody galahs, so I'll be calling out the team numbers in strict order, starting with . . . *Team 1!*'

As Shagger, the PC of Team 1, stepped forward to collect his map, Jimbo leaned sideways to whisper to Red, 'What the fuck's a galah?'

'A dumb cunt,' Red whispered back. 'Jesus, you Poms are pig-ignorant!'

The rest of the PCs were called out in strict order of teams to collect their maps from the sergeant-major. Once each PC had received his map, he led the other three members of his team to the armoury tent, where they collect a GPMG, a SARBE communications-rescue beacon, and either an A510 or PRC 64 radio, or a USAF PRC 47 high-frequency radio transceiver. When the man acting as signaller had humped his radio on to his back, on top of his bergen, the separate components of the GPMG, including barrel and tripod, were divided among the other three men. Then all four men returned to the parade ground for a final briefing from Callaghan.

'I want each PC to open his map and study it now. You'll be leaving the base via the patrol route exit and I want you to take your bearings from that – it's clearly marked on the map. The PC will carry the map on his person at all times, along with the SARBE, but we're allowing ten minutes for the other men to study it as well and get a rough idea of his allotted area of reconnaissance. Also marked on the map is the patrol area of your backup team. Memorize that as well. Bear in mind that once the patrol starts, you won't be coming back in until the whole perimeter has been cleared and Line

Alpha established and secured. Bear in mind, also, that although you may at times feel isolated, our choppers will be right above you for reconnaissance, resups and casevacs, and you can contact them at any time by SARBE. Your PCs can also contact Operational Control back here on the base. Now if anyone wants to have a last cigarette while his PC studies the map, go ahead. You have ten minutes before you move out, so make the most of it.'

The PCs pored over their maps while the other men smoked or chewed gum. Then each gathered his men around him, laid the map on the ground, and let them study it for ten minutes. This done, and questions asked and answered, the PCs stood up and led their four-man teams, in strict numerical order, out of the base.

Moving out in file formation, as would all the rest, Team 1 was the first to depart. The sun was now high in the sky, but burning through gathering clouds as the teams dispersed into the paddy-fields, rubber plantations and dense jungle surrounding the camp.

7

Team 1, followed almost immediately by Team 2, marched carefully along the camouflaged, almost invisible patrol route exit, between the claymores buried on either side. Up ahead on point, Dead-eye held his SLR across his chest and kept his eyes on the ground, taking note from the flattened grass exactly where the patrol route exit lay. The mines, he knew, had been carefully concealed and came right up to both sides of the jungle path, so that one wrong step in either direction and a man could be blown to hell. Strung out in single file behind Dead-eye, the other three men were also on the alert, with Shagger second in line as PC, and Red behind him as signaller, both covering an arc of fire on both sides of the trail, and placing emphasis on studying the shadowy spaces between the rubber trees that came up to the very edge of the minefields. Last in line, as Tail-end Charlie, Jimbo also studied both sides of the path, though once out of the mined area and off the exit route, he would be compelled to constantly turn around and cover their rear.

Negotiating the mines was always a nerve-racking business, but luckily it didn't take long. A few minutes later the four men had reached the end of the exit and were able to breathe more easily as they knelt together in the shade of the rubber trees. There, as Team 2 could be seen making their way cautiously along the hidden pathway, Shagger checked his map again for the direction they would have to take to their selected patrol area, while the other three camouflaged the equipment they had picked up in the armoury, including the PRC 64 radio set and the separate parts of the GPMG. As they were moving off again, in a direction indicated silently by Shagger's hand signal, Team 2 was coming off the exit route. This time, the two groups of men did not shout jokes at one another, but remained totally silent. Shagger indicated with another hand signal the direction his team was to take. Then they moved off.

As they turned east into the nearest rubber plantation, they passed from fierce sunlight to deep gloom and appalling humidity. Instantly, they started sweating and the air around them filled up with clouds of mosquitoes and midges. Tormented by both the sweat dripping into their eyes and the attacking insects, they had to force themselves to study the shadows intently, Dead-eye concentrating on the front, Shagger and Red covering both sides, and Jimbo now in the stressful position of having to repeatedly turn around to cover their rear, as well as covering his two sides. Spaced well apart to prevent the whole team being hit by the same burst of enemy gunfire, they soon felt acutely aware of their isolation from one another and could not prevent the tension building up in them.

The deeper they went into the jungle, the gloomier and more humid it became, with the rubber trees often giving way to secondary vegetation that was a seemingly impenetrable tangle of shrubs, vines, and overhanging, intertwining branches bearing huge palm leaves that could slice open the skin without the victim feeling it. As both the ground beneath their feet and the overhanging branches could conceal snakes and poisonous spiders, they were compelled to inspect these carefully as they marched. They also had to check above and below for booby-traps. This need for caution slowed them down considerably and placed an even greater strain upon them. In addition, the jungle contained many narrow streams which had to be crossed and which, being exposed areas, were natural ambush positions for the enemy.

The jungle was not silent, for there was the ceaseless rustling of breeze-blown leaves, the scurrying of animals in the under-growth, the flapping of birds, the chattering of monkeys and the babbling of streams. To make listening for the enemy even more difficult, these sounds, which the men were gradually becoming accustomed to filtering out, were repeatedly drowned by the deep rumble of bombers, the screeching of jets, or the whap-whapping of helicopters passing overhead. Their only consolation on hearing this din was the fact that some of those choppers were their own reconnaissance craft on the lookout for the enemy.

When they had passed through the rubber plantation and into the impenetrable foliage of secondary forest, their progress slowed even more as they had to hack their way through the undergrowth with machetes. This was sweat-inducing, back-breaking work, but, because it was so noisy, it was also dangerous. This combination of agonizing work, snail's-pace progress and constant awareness of danger was, even for experienced men, both draining and disheartening, and the wearier they grew the more demoralized they felt. They were therefore glad when, two hours later, yet only one mile on, they emerged from the jungle's gloom to the hotter, brighter and less humid open space of a broad paddy-field.

At the edge of the jungle Shagger dropped to one knee and hand-signalled that they should all do the same. When they had done so and were partially hidden by the stalks of bamboo and tall grass, Shagger studied the paddy-field through his green binoculars, seeing only the tall grass rippling like the waves of a bright-green sea, with shimmering heat waves rising eerily off it. He studied that expanse of grass for a long time, trying to see, in the constant, wave-like motion, a different kind of motion that would reveal the presence of the VC. Eventually, satisfied that the field was empty, he lowered the binoculars, used the PRC 64 to contact HQ and inform them of the team's whereabouts, then waved his hand in a forward motion.

The four men moved forward at the half crouch, weapons held at the ready, their eyes scanning the waving bamboo and grass on all sides of them. The sinking sun was obliterated by the dark clouds that still filled the sky, pregnant with rain. Occasionally, above the clouds, they could hear the reassuring beat of the Iroquois helicopters of No. 9 Squadron RAAF, flying in from Vung Tau to give them support with aerial reconnaissance and anything else required.

Then the rain came.

They were only halfway across the paddy-field when the clouds burst and, accompanied by thunder and lightning, unleashed on them a seemingly interminable downpour. Within seconds they were all drenched; within minutes they were forced to their knees and hiding under their ponchos as the water in the paddy-fields rose up to cover their thighs. The rain hammering on the ponchos over their heads sounded like deafening jungle drums.

Suddenly bullets stitched the field all around them, making the water spurt up in angry, jagged lines that formed arcs all around them and rapidly moved in closer.

'Down!' Shagger bellowed, dropping to one knee, which disappeared in the water, and raising his automatic rifle to the firing position and squinting along the sight.

'Where the fuck are they?' Red asked, looking ahead, then left and right, watching the water spitting up mere feet away, but inching closer to him.

'Shoot and scoot!' Dead-eye called out, then started wading away from the sizzling water while firing short bursts from his SLR in the direction of the enemy gunfire.

'Bug out!' Shagger bawled. '*Bug out!*'

Dead-eye, however, retreated only a short distance from where the enemy bullets were peppering the watery paddy-field and then, still firing his SLR, began circling around the field of fire, which was still directed at the other three men. Once out of its range, he slung the SLR over his shoulder, jerked an M26 hand-grenade from his webbing and hurled it with all his might. He was now in shallow water and even as the grenade was arcing down towards the enemy ambush position he ran towards it, firing his rifle from the hip. The grenade exploded with a thunderclap that created a fountain of water, bamboo, smouldering grass and smoke, followed by the high-pitched screams of wounded men.

It stopped the hail of enemy gunfire. As Dead-eye ran towards the VC position, still shooting from the hip, Shagger, Red and Jimbo followed suit, all pouring a relentless fusillade into the spiralling column of smoke. Dead-eye reached the position first, splashing out of the shallow water and running up on to muddy ground, firing into the guerrillas he saw in the remains of their hide, some dead, some still alive, the latter still dazed from the blast of the grenade and groping frantically, blindly, for their weapons.

Dead-eye poured a final burst into the man nearest to him just as the other three members of the team raced in from the other side, all firing at once. The VC hide turned into a convulsion of exploding bamboo and grass, flying tatters of bloody camouflaged cloth, geysering mud and soil, as the frail, dark-skinned men in black fatigues and black felt hats shuddered violently and were punched to the ground, soaked in their own blood.

While Shagger, Red and Jimbo were checking that the VC were all dead, Dead-eye was up and out of the hide to reconnoitre the area for other hides or individual guerrillas. He found none. Returning to the devastated hide, which was now a mess of blood-soaked bodies and charred vegetation, he found Red and Jimbo, who had inspected the bloody corpses, looking for maps or other valuable scraps of information, while Shagger was on the radio, calling for an OP team to be inserted and replace the dead VC. Receiving confirmation, he then called Team 2 to establish their whereabouts. Learning that they were in their allotted area of patrol, though had so far made no contact with the enemy, he gave details of his own position and then killed the communication. The rain was still pouring down.

'What a bloody mess,' he murmured, glancing about him at the low, sullen sky, the merciless rain, the pools of water clouded with orange mud, the dead Viet Cong, most of whom looked like adolescents, lying in pools of blood, their uniforms lacerated and their smashed ribs and other bones exposed. 'That's all we needed.'

'We didn't need it,' Dead-eye replied, 'but that's what we got. It's no big deal, Sarge.'

'There speaks the British SAS,' said Red. 'Let me bow down and kiss his boots.'

'Are we clear, Dead-eye?' Shagger asked, ignoring his mate's sarcasm.

'Yep.'

'Then we'll sit here and hold this position until the replacement team gets here.'

With no choice in the matter, the four men squatted around the devastated hide, their backs turned to the corpses inside, their eyes scanning the rain-drenched paddy-field in all directions. After about twenty minutes an Iroquois appeared through the murk and was soon roaring right above them, its rotors sweeping the rain around it in glistening sheets. First out when it landed were the 5th Battalion soldiers who would take over the VC hide and hold it as an Australian OP. Next out were the medics, who set about lifting the dead guerrillas on to stretchers and carrying them into the chopper for transfer to a burial site outside Vung Tau. Once the bodies had been removed, the men from the 5th Battalion began modifying the hide for their own purposes. As they were doing so, the chopper took off and Shagger's patrol waved goodbye, wished the soldiers good luck and marched on.

Heading east, eventually they left the paddy-field and started weaving between the soaring trees of another rubber plantation. The rain had now stopped and the heat of the sun returned, casting striations of light on the jungle floor and making steam rise from the soaked vegetation. Soon, the humidity was once again unbearable, making all the men drip sweat, while whining mosquitos and hordes of no less aggressive insects returned to assail them.

As usual, they were marching in single file and it was Deadeye, out on point, who saw a slight movement high in a tree up ahead and bawled a warning as the first shot rang out. He was already diving to the side of the narrow track when the bullet thudded into the ground where he had been walking.

Crashing through the undergrowth and rolling on to his belly, he aimed at where he had seen the movement and fired a short burst from his SLR, raking the barrel up and down, left to right, to ensure that he hit the unseen sniper. Leaves and branches were blown apart, raining to the ground. They were followed by a rifle, then the man fell screaming, smashing his way down through the branches to thud into the earth.

As Dead-eye jumped to his feet to advance again, more bullets whined past him and ricocheted off the nearby trees. Instantly, the combined weapons of Shagger, Jimbo and Red roared into action behind him, tearing the trees to shreds high up where the first sniper had been. Another guerrilla plunged to earth, his body breaking the branches as he fell.

Dead-eye was weaving through the trees, advancing, even before the VC hit the ground. In fact, the dead man thudded into the ground just as Dead-eye reached the trunk of the tree and raised his SLR to fire vertically, directly above him. The branches were torn to shreds, raining leaves and wood splinters, then another black-clad body crashed down, screaming, bouncing off the thick branches, smashing through the thin ones. Dead-eye stepped aside just in time, letting the bloody, mangled body thud into the earth where he had been standing. As he glanced up it was clear to him that no more snipers were hidden in that particular tree.

There was the sound of rushing feet, then Shagger and the other two were standing beside him, all breathless.

'Any more?' Shagger asked.

'Yes, I think so,' Dead-eye told him. 'I suspect there's a whole nest of them up in these trees. This bit of jungle is on high ground and they must have a wonderful view from the top of the trees to our base camp, so I think a lot of the sniping's been done from there.'

'Which means we have to get out of here and then get this area levelled completely.'

'Correct,' Dead-eye said. 'Bomb it all to hell, then take it over and use it as our own FOB.'

Shagger glanced at Red and grinned. 'A right little angel of mercy. I thought the English were soft, Red.'

'Not this bastard,' Red said. 'Just take a look at his fucking eyes: they're as dead as chopped liver.'

'Do we do it or not?' Dead-eye asked, neither amused nor offended by Red's remark.

'I say we do it,' Red told him.

'So do I,' Jimbo said.

'OK, let's do it, Shagger agreed. 'Every man for himself.'

'Then we need an RV at the other side of the jungle,' Dead-eye reminded him.

Shagger nodded and removed from his pocket the map, which he unfolded and held so that the other three, now bunched around him, could see it. After checking their present position, he jabbed at a point on the map some two hundred yards south of the far side of the jungle. 'There,' he said. 'Between the jungle and the next VC position, which is a bunker complex. If we get separated on our way through the jungle, we make our way to that location and from there call in air support to clear this lot out.' He folded the map and placed it back in his pocket, then said, 'So, let's do it.'

'Who goes first?' Red asked.

'Me,' Shagger said. 'If I draw their fire, you may be able to see them and take some of them out. When I get out of the trees, I'll give you covering fire and you'll each do the same in turn. Best of luck, piss-pots.'

Shagger carefully scanned the jungle around them, took a deep breath, then ran out from the cover of the immediate group of trees and raced away, crouched low and swerving left to right with his M16A1 automatic rifle at the ready. He had scarcely gone twenty yards when a sniper all in black rose from behind some bushes and took aim with an AK47 assault rifle. Instantly, Dead-eye leaned out of the side of his tree and fired a short, noisy burst that sent the man spinning back into the bushes. Other VC appeared, popping up from the foliage or craning out from behind the trees ahead of Shagger as he weaved left and right, always keeping a tree between him and the enemy.

Dead-eye, Jimbo and Red were now firing in turn, each picking a separate target, attempting to keep the VC pinned down until Shagger, who had veered around them to the right, was clear of their field of fire and heading for the far end of the jungle. When he reached the edge of the trees unhurt, he threw himself to the ground, rolled over on to his belly and fired at the backs of the VC, thus creating a withering crossfire.

Jimbo advanced next, following Shagger's course, firing his SLR from the hip as he darted from one tree to another, gradually making his way forward under the covering fire of his friends, front and rear. Though the VC were mostly pinned down, they still managed to fire a lot of shots, their bullets ricocheting noisily off tree trunks and branches, showering Jimbo in flying foliage as he ran.

Racing across a small clearing, through streaks of brilliant sunlight and pools of ink-black shadow, he was stopped in his tracks when a trapdoor suddenly popped open in the ground just in front of him. As grass and leaves slid off the trapdoor, which was made of bamboo, a yellow face came into view, one eye squinting along the sights of an AK47.

Not stopping for a second, though scarcely believing what he was seeing, Jimbo jumped over the man's head even as he fired his first shot. The combined guns of Dead-eye and Red resounded behind Jimbo as he ran on. Glancing back over his shoulder, he saw the bloody, shattered head of the

VC sinking back down through the hole like a pomegranate smashed open with a hammer.

Still not too sure if he had seen right, Jimbo ran out, darting from tree to tree, firing from the hip at the shadowy figures he saw popping up from the undergrowth or leaning out from the trees. Then he hurled himself to the ground at the edge of the jungle, rolling on to his belly a few yards from Shagger.

'Bloody hell!' he exclaimed. 'That bastard came up out of the ground!'

'Like a trapdoor spider,' Shagger replied. 'They just raise the lid as you pass over and – whammo! – they've got you.'

'A tunnel complex?'

'Maybe. They're all over the bloody place. More likely, though, that was just an individual sniper in a camouflaged hide. Now shut up and start firing.'

Lying beside Shagger, Jimbo opened fire with his SLR, shredding the jungle ahead, where, in a dark-green sea of exploding foliage, he saw a group of VC, some facing Red and Dead-eye, the others frantically turning around to deal with this fresh gunfire from their rear.

'*Go!*' Dead-eye bawled at Red and the Australian hurled himself forward, heavily burdened with his bulky radio but still managing to weave left and right, dashing from one tree to another as bullets ricocheted off the trunks and branches, spitting lumps of bark and wood at him. Giving covering fire from the front, Dead-eye fired his SLR in short, savage, devastatingly accurate bursts, picking off a guerrilla the instant one exposed the slightest part of himself.

Red, meanwhile, was weaving through a hail of bullets and flying foliage, first left, then right, frequently hugging a tree trunk until Dead-eye's fire from his rear and the combined fusillade from his two friends in front had once more forced the enemy to lie low. Eventually, following the route taken by the others, he made it to the far side of the trees and knelt beside his two friends. After adjusting the cumbersome radio on his back, he lay belly down beside the others.

'There's more fucking VC than mosquitoes in there,' he said. 'A right fucking nest of them.'

'If Dead-eye makes it,' Shagger replied, 'we'll wipe out that whole stretch of jungle. Blow it all to hell. Here he comes. Start firing.'

Dead-eye moved with the speed and cunning he had picked up in the jungles of Malaya and Borneo, running crouched as low as he could get, weaving from side to side, sometimes throwing himself to the ground and rolling behind a tree, while bullets from the guerrillas' AK47s thudded into the soil, bounced off tree trunks and showered him with shredded foliage and bark. As he advanced, his three friends kept up a barrage of gunfire from their combination of SLRs and M16A1s, eventually forcing most of the VC to turn away from Dead-eye and defend their rear. This enabled Dead-eye to make the last of his run around the enemy position, pass it and eventually reach a position parallel with his friends, though a good distance away.

'Bug out!' Shagger bawled.

Even as the others were rising to make their tactical retreat, Dead-eye was hurling an M26 hand-grenade at the VC who had dared to advance out of their hide. The grenade exploded in their midst, blowing some of them into the air, dazing others, and showering the living and the dead with raining debris as the branches of nearby trees caught fire and black smoke billowed up. Dead-eye hurled a second grenade as his three friends raced through the trees on the edge of the jungle, all heading off obliquely in different directions, firing on the run, intending to circle back and meet each other at the RV already agreed upon. As they were disappearing, Dead-eye raked the VC still moving in their devastated, smoke-obscured hide, then he too turned and raced away.

He did not have to run far. A couple of hundred yards beyond the trees, in a raised, dry stretch of monsoon drain that ran alongside another paddy-field, Shagger, Red and Jimbo were sprawled near each other, trying to get their breath back. When Dead-eye slithered down beside them, they continued breathing deeply for a while, soon started breathing normally, then at last sat up.

'That was a close one,' Jimbo said.

'Too close,' Shagger replied. 'And that bit of jungle is crawling with Charlie, so let's level the bastard. Red, get me HQ.' Red removed the radio from his back, placed it on the dry floor of the monsoon drain, contacted HQ, then handed Shagger the microphone. Checking his opened map, Shagger ordered gun support and an airstrike, followed by a body-removal team and troop insertion by chopper to enable the wooded hill to be held. He finished by giving the grid location, then cut the transmission and handed the microphone back to Red. 'Thirty minutes,' he said. 'If you drongos want a smoke or a brew-up, you can have it now. I'll get up on the rim of this monsoon drain and guide the aircraft in with the SARBE. Bring me a cuppa and a bar of chocolate, Red.'

'Will do,' Red said. He was already unpacking his stove from his bergen as Shagger unclipped his SARBE beacon from his webbing and crawled up the sloping concrete side of the drain. After reaching the top, he remained on his belly while scanning the surrounding terrain with binoculars. He then surveyed the sky with his naked eye. Meanwhile, Red had set alight the hexamine blocks beneath his portable stove and was collecting a metal cup from each man. By now he had a cigarette between his lips, as had Jimbo, and both were puffing away with great pleasure. When the water had boiled, Red dropped a tea bag into each cup and poured on hot water. While the tea was brewing, each man, with the exception of Shagger, tucked into whatever cold, high-calorie rations took his fancy, which meant either chocolate or dried biscuits and cheese. Red handed up a mug of steaming tea to Shagger, followed by his requested bar of chocolate. All four men then settled back to wait for the gun bombardment, with Shagger eating his chocolate and sipping his tea while he scanned the western sky.

Exactly thirty minutes later, when all other Task Force teams had been ordered by radio to clear the area, the New Zealanders' battery of 105mm guns opened fire from Nui Dat. The distant thump-thump of the opening barrage was followed almost immediately by the ever louder whistling of the incoming shells, then the tree-covered hill to the west erupted in an inferno of soaring flames, billowing black smoke, and a rain of soil, stones, burning branches and shredded, smouldering foliage. This hellish devastation continued for what seemed like an eternity, though in fact it was only fifteen minutes. By the time it ended the summit of the hill – or what could be seen of it through the slowly spiralling smoke – was denuded of trees and seemed no more than a smouldering black crater.

When the smoke cleared there were in fact still trees left on the summit, though they were charred as black as the hilltop and completely stripped of branches. By contrast, the lower slopes were still dense with trees, and undoubtedly more VC were lurking there, either above or below ground.

For this reason, the 105mm bombardment was followed by six USAF Phantom Jet F-4Cs which, guided in by Shagger's beacon, barrelled down from the sky to release a salvo of rockets. The exploding napalm formed vivid balls of fire that appeared to roll down the hill like boiling lava under billowing black smoke. The remaining trees burst into flames and these in turn torched more trees until the whole hill, beneath its charred summit, was a fearsome, dazzling furnace that resembled an overflowing volcano.

When the American jet fighters had departed, the flames burned for two more hours, covering the hills with a dreadful pall of oily black smoke. Eventually, when the smoke cleared away, the lower hill had been stripped of foliage and the remaining trees, bare of branches and charred black, were still smouldering.

Shortly afterwards, eight RAAF Iroquois helicopters emerged from the north and descended over the cratered summit of the hill, their noisy rotors whipping up great clouds of soil and black dust. Dangling on ropes below one of the choppers was a D6 bulldozer. Released before the other helicopters had landed, the bulldozer drifted down on eight parachutes and landed softly on one side of the devastated summit. The other choppers then landed one by one, great slugs in the swirling black dust, and disgorged the 6th Battalion troops who would arrange for the burial of the VC dead and then take over the hill, turning it into a forward operating base and defensive position that would give an invaluable view of the lowlands around it.

Even as Shagger and the other three SAS men clambered to their feet and prepared to march off, the bulldozer had begun the job of pushing up tons of scorched soil and the dead that littered it, to create a mass grave. By the time the

SAS four-man team had scrambled out of the monsoon drain and continued their march south, the cratered hill, though still covered with what looked like coal dust, was a hive of activity, the many Australian soldiers resembling ghosts in the murk.

It was a vision from some terrible dream.

8

The smouldering hill had scarcely dropped out of sight when Red received a message from Team 2's PC, Sergeant Don Ingrams, informing him that he and his men were a mile further north-east and had just come up against a VC platoon ensconced in a camouflaged bunker complex. They needed urgent help. Ingrams had already called for air support and more men, but he was told that no fighters or helicopters would be available for at least another hour – ironically, many had been used to assist Team 1 at the hill they had just taken – and he needed Team 1 to help him out immediately. Ingrams gave Red the grid reference, warned him to watch out for minefields and booby-traps, then rang off even before saying, 'Over and out.'

'He must be pinned down,' Red suggested, replacing the radio's microphone on its hook. 'He sounded pretty desperate.'

'Let's get going,' Shagger said.

The first part of the march took them across the open paddy-field, where they all felt particularly exposed. They marched in the usual single file, but spaced even farther apart than usual. Dead-eye, on point, advanced with extreme caution, keeping his SLR at the ready and carefully scanning the ground for the smallest sign of a booby-trap or mine. This task was rendered even more nerve-racking by the fact that the soft soil of the paddy-field was covered by shallow, muddy water that obscured what lay on the bottom. Also, the paddy-field was devoid of trees or any other kind of shelter, which meant they could only fall belly down should the VC open fire.

Troubled by this risk, after about thirty minutes of laborious wading Shagger momentarily stopped the advance and used the radio to call in a RAAF surveillance helicopter. Waiting for the chopper to arrive, the men were forced to kneel in the shallow water, each facing a point of the compass and each straining to see any unusual movement other than the gentle undulations of the tall grass blown by a warm wind. As usual, that warm wind provided scant relief from the humidity, which made them break out in sweat; nor were they spared the attentions of countless frantic insects.

'I can take anything but these fuckers,' Red informed the others, swotting desperately at the cloud of mosquitoes whining about his face. 'The VC, their booby-traps, their bloody tunnels – anything but these bastards.'

'They don't bother me,' replied Jimbo, merely shaking his head to rid himself of the insects biting at him. 'But then I'm in the *British* SAS. I'm not a ball-and-chain migrant.'

'I'm no bloody immigrant,' Red snapped. 'I was born and raised in Australia, mate, and don't you forget it.'

'How can I forget it,' Jimbo retorted, 'when you talk like that?'

'Don't give me that kind of snobbery, you Pommie ponce. At least I speak. You just vomit . . .'

'Shut up, you pair of drongos,' Shagger broke in. 'I think I just heard the chopper.'

He was right. After what had seemed like an interminable ten minutes, when their legs had started aching from the strain of kneeling in shallow water, an RAAF Iroquois, converted to a gunship, appeared on the horizon, flying at low level across paddy-fields and jungle, clearly searching for Charlie as it approached. Framed by drifting clouds streaked with sunlight, it hovered above them, whipping up a wind, while Shagger transmitted the team's position with his SARBE. When the pilot dropped even lower to eyeball Shagger's position, the gunner sitting behind one of the heavy machine-guns waved at the team, letting them know he had seen them. The chopper ascended vertically to about 300 feet, hovered for a few seconds, then flew north-east at low level, reconnoitring the paddy-field ahead of the men on the ground.

Though the field looked absolutely empty, the pilot had obviously seen something below him, since he suddenly slowed down, circled back, then ascended low enough for the wind created by the rotors to violently whip the tall grass and bamboo stalks.

Suddenly bursts of AK47 automatic rifle fire were unleashed from the paddy-field, clearly aimed upward at the chopper, which ascended rapidly, vertically, with its heavy machine-guns roaring into action, returning the gunfire coming from the VC position directly below it.

'Charlie straight ahead!' Shagger bawled, jabbing his finger towards the VC ambush position.

Even as Shagger was shouting, the roar of a Soviet 7.6 mm RPD light machine-gun started up from the ambush position and a fusillade of bullets caused spitting water and mud to race in a snaking line towards the SAS team. Already scattering, the four men threw themselves to the watery ground and rolled away even farther as the line of bullets stitched its way between them and raced on. As the men rolled on to their bellies and took aim, they saw a black-clad guerrilla rising to his knees and squinting along the sights of the RPG7 rocket-propelled grenade launcher resting on his shoulder.

'*Grenade!*' Jimbo bawled.

Smoke belched from the rear of the Soviet-made grenade launcher, the rocket shot out on spitting flame and smoke, and the guerrilla was still recoiling from the backblast when the missile, completing its high arc, screeched down to explode with a deafening roar mere yards from the SAS men, tearing up the earth and showering them with soil and water.

Even as Shagger, Red and Jimbo were either slapping their ears to get their hearing back or wiping soil from their eyes, Dead-eye was rising to his knees, taking aim with his SLR, and firing a brief, savage burst that first made the earth spit and swirl around the VC, then threw him into convulsions and finally punched him back into the tall grass, with the grenade launcher spilling from his hands. Another guerrilla was crawling forward to pick up the grenade launcher when the RAAF helicopter descended to rake the VC position with a lethal combination of rockets and heavy machine-guns.

'*Advance!*' Shagger bawled.

The machine-guns of the Iroquois were pouring a hail of bullets into the mushrooming soil and smoke created by the helicopter's rockets when the other three SAS troopers jumped to their feet and ran forward at the crouch, spreading out in a broad arc that would enable them to encircle the ambush position ahead. Still in touch with the RAAF helicopter by means of his SARBE, Shagger learnt, just before the chopper ascended again out of range of the VC guns, that though the main ambush party had been decimated, one soldier had managed to get his hands on the grenade launcher and the few other VC were still in command of their RPD light machine-gun.

'We'll handle it,' Shagger said.

Using a hand signal, he indicated that the others should spread out and continue their advance on the area now clearly marked by burning brush and swirling clouds of smoke. The men did so, crouching low and moving slowly, keeping their eyes peeled for mines and booby-traps. This made their progress agonizingly slow.

Nevertheless, the smoke from the burning brush continued spiralling up ahead and eventually they found themselves entering that grey haze. Just before the haze thickened, Shagger used more hand signals to silently indicate that the men were to split up and operate as individuals until contact with the enemy had been made. Each man signalled back that he understood, then they spread out again and began their stealthy encirclement of the ambush position, from which not a sound could be heard.

It was eerie in the smoke. Because the wind had dropped, the smoke was both drifting and clearing very slowly. The ambush position had been located at the far edge of the paddy-field, close to the next stretch of jungle, where the VC bunker complex was dug in, and the stooped palm leaves and branches of the trees could be discerned slightly beyond the smoke, sometimes moving almost imperceptibly, like ghosts in a mist.

This was all the more disconcerting in that the smoke made it difficult to determine the difference between shapes created by the jungle foliage beyond the smoke and what may have been human figures trying to stay as still as possible in the ambush position at the edge of the paddy-field.

Now isolated from one another, advancing through the dense smoke, desperately trying to make no noise that would disturb the unnatural silence, each of the four SAS men had his personal moment of doubt, realizing that each second might be his last.

Though still concentrating hard on what he was doing, Shagger couldn't help thinking briefly of his wife and two children back in Woodvale, Western Australia, where they lived in a bungalow in a neat green suburb. His recollection of his home was unexpected and vivid, rushing into his head with memories of barbecues in the back garden, cycling with the kids, trips to the sea and the waterfront of Swanbourne, where Shagger kept a small boat for family trips into the Indian Ocean. All of that could end very soon if Charlie opened fire first.

The recollection of barbecues on long summer evenings had almost certainly been conjured up by the smell of the smoke through which Shagger was now so carefully making his way. When he realized that his thoughts were wandering, he jerked himself back to the present, focusing even more intently on what was happening around him.

Had something just moved up ahead?

Red, on the other hand, had no family to be concerned with, other than an ailing mother in Chatswood, Sydney, whom he tried to think about as little as possible because she was such a headache to him. But now she came back to his thoughts, as he felt himself tensing, waiting for the sudden roar of an AK47 and the bullet that would strike him down for good.

Red had been only twelve when his father had died. His main recollection of his life with his mother since then was of her being constantly ill and him looking after her. He'd had to do everything: clean the house, do the washing, go shopping, cook for her, feed her, make her bed, deal with her bedpan and sometimes, when she was particularly ill, bathe her. To make matters worse, she was cranky, endlessly demanding, and showed little appreciation of his efforts. By the time Red was eighteen he hated his mother with passion; not least because he had come to see clearly that looking after her had deprived him of a private life. In truth, he had joined the army just to get away from her, leaving her in the care of the social services. Then, once signed up, he had made up for all he had lost, boozing with his mates and screwing around while avoiding truly close relationships with women – until he had met Mildred. Red had only wanted his freedom.

Now, as he advanced at the crouch through the smoke, his weapon at the ready, he had a brief vision of his mother ill in bed, purple-faced, nagging him, and he found himself wondering, with a certain satisfaction, what she would do if he copped it from a VC bullet within the next few minutes.

He was brought abruptly back to reality when he saw something moving ahead . . .

Also advancing stealthily through the smoke, looking out simultaneously for mines, booby-traps and VC hiding at ground level, Jimbo found himself thinking that if he died in this action it would be particularly ironic. For this was, he had suddenly remembered, his penultimate operation in the field. After three decades of active service in North Africa, Europe, Oman, Malaya, Borneo, Aden and now here, age was taking its toll and his time was fast running out. Indeed, just before coming here he had been informed by Lieutenant-Colonel Callaghan that if he survived this tour in Vietnam he would be sent back to Aden and the Radfan for his final campaign – indeed, the final British campaign in that country. After that, he would be transferred to a teaching job in the Training Wing at Hereford.

Jimbo found it hard to believe that he was now that old, but the fact had to be faced. Yet even as he accepted it, he realized that he couldn't bear the thought of a teaching job, always being stuck in Hereford, and that he wanted to keep fighting for ever. Copping a bullet in the next minute or two might not be a bad thing, he decided. Go out with a bang, mate.

Then something or someone moved up ahead. A shadowy form in the still dense, drifting smoke, rising up from the ground.

Jimbo brought his SLR down from the cross position and raised it to take aim . . .

Dead-eye, being a lot younger than Jimbo, but still widely experienced and a born killing machine, was the one man in the team who had no thought for anything other than the instant. Concentrating like an animal only on what could be seen and heard in the dense smoke – including the ground, where booby-traps might be waiting to spike his foot or blow his legs off – all his senses were narrowly focused and ready to respond to any situation. It was therefore probably no accident that in the instant the others either sensed or saw something ahead, Dead-eye was the first to realize that the almost imperceptible movement of a shadowy form in the smoke was not the trembling of a palm leaf or branch in the breeze, but the stealthy movement of an undernourished human being slowly standing upright.

No, that wasn't a shivering palm leaf or branch – it was a weapon, some kind of rifle, being lowered and aimed.

'*VC!*' Dead-eye bawled and then fired his SLR, raking the area straight ahead.

A Russian RPD light machine-gun roared in response.

Dead-eye was on the ground, on his belly, when the hail of bullets whistled and whined through the air. As the enemy machine-gun continued roaring, he saw a tiny yellow-blue flame in the murk, spitting out smoke that was blacker than the smoke still rising from the smouldering bamboo and grass. Glancing back over his shoulder, he saw that the other three had also gone to ground and were slithering backwards into a hollow that promised some protection. Once there, they began setting up the tripod for the GPMG.

Hoping to draw the VC fire and keep them distracted, Dead-eye opened up again with his SLR, firing at the slightest sign of movement. Someone screamed in the murk, but his cry of pain was followed by the unmistakable thudding sound of the grenade launcher.

The ground erupted near Dead-eye, temporarily deafening him with its roaring, pummelling him with the blast, and showering him with loose soil, stones, bamboo and smouldering grass.

Shaking his head from side to side, trying to clear it of ringing sounds, he glanced ahead and saw the shadowy form of a man with something long and thin balanced on his shoulder – the RPG7. Dead-eye took aim and fired. The man screamed and convulsed, then dropped his weapon as he was punched to the ground and disappeared in smoke.

The GPMG roared into action behind Dead-eye as Jimbo raked the VC position with a savage, sustained burst. The instant he saw that chaos of spitting soil, stones, bamboo and shredded leaves around the shadowy forms of the VC in the smoke, Dead-eye was up and running, firing his SLR from the hip.

Within seconds Shagger and Red had done the same, racing out in opposite directions and circling around to come back in on the VC position from opposite sides, forming a triangular pincer movement with Dead-eye, who was coming up from the front. Imagining that they were surrounded by a superior force, the VC panicked and started turning every which way, firing blindly through the swirling smoke.

Just before reaching the lip of the VC hide, Dead-eye lobbed a hand grenade that fell between the man trying to adjust the elevation of the grenade launcher and the RPD light machine-gun crew, who had clearly just seen the advancing Shagger and were swinging the barrel of their weapon towards him. The explosion tore the VC position to shreds, obscuring them in smoke, and its roaring was followed by the dreadful cries of those still alive. Darting up on to the rim of the hide while the debris from the blast was still raining down, Dead-eye fired a series of short, precise bursts down into the position, at anyone he saw moving. Within seconds, Shagger and Red were doing the same, taking no chances, turning the smoky hide into a nightmare of spitting soil and stones, writhing limbs, screams, entreaties and dying moans. They stopped firing before their magazines were empty, then looked down at their handiwork.

'We got them all,' Dead-eye said with satisfaction, staring into that smoky hell. 'Not even a wounded man left. Not a twitch down there.'

'Bloody hell,' Red whispered, amazed at Dead-eye's icy remove and realizing, at last, that he wasn't dealing with a pair of soft Brits, but with at least one truly hard man and another, less cold but still tough and fearless.

Glancing at Shagger, he saw that he too was glancing from the dead men in the smouldering hide to Dead-eye, obviously thinking the same. Finally, letting his breath out in what sounded like a sigh, Shagger asked, 'Is the radio back there with Jimbo?'

'Yeah,' Red said. 'As he was manning the GPMG, I left the radio with him.'

'OK. Let's go back and join him,' Shagger said and turned to Dead-eye. 'I'm going to call HQ and ask for men to take over this hide. While I'm doing that, you check the area between here and the edge of that jungle.'

'Can do,' Dead-eye said. He strode off and melted into the thinning smoke, heading in the direction of the jungle where Team 2 were presently engaged in conflict with a VC bunker complex. Even before he had disappeared, Shagger had set off in the opposite direction to rejoin Jimbo. Knowing that the battle for the VC hide had ended, Jimbo was already dismantling the GPMG and tripod, in preparation for the march into the jungle in support of Team 2.

Kneeling beside him, Red switched on the radio, contacted HQ, then passed the microphone to Shagger, who asked for the usual burial detail and enough replacements to turn the captured VC hide into an OP and defensive position.

No sooner had Shagger handed the microphone back to Red than the latter received an incoming message from Ingrams, asking when Team 1 could be expected and sounding more desperate.

'We'll have to wait here for the replacements to arrive,' Shagger replied dispassionately, 'but we should be there in half an hour. You surrounded?'

'No. It's just that we can't get past them. There's what seems like a whole platoon of the bastards, dug into an extensive bunker complex. We can hardly lift our faces out of the dirt; we're well and truly pinned down. We urgently need your support.'

'Keep your faces in the dirt,' Shagger recommended laconically, 'and we'll be along as soon as possible.'

'Fair enough,' Ingrams said, sounding relieved. 'Over and out.'

Shagger cut the transmission and handed the receiver back to Red. Having just finished dismantling the GPMG, Jimbo glanced about him, wanting to know what was happening. 'Where's Dead-eye?' he asked.

Shagger jerked his thumb back over his shoulder. 'Checking that there are no more VC between here and the jungle.'

'If there are, God help them,' Jimbo replied.

'Too right. That's some animal.'

'He's no animal,' Jimbo told him. 'He's just a damn good soldier. He's been through things you couldn't even imagine, mate, that's why he's so quiet. He doesn't show his emotions.'

'What couldn't I imagine?' Shagger asked him.

'The Telok Anson swamp in Malaya,' Jimbo replied. 'That's something you couldn't imagine unless you've been through it.'

'When you've been in a tunnel complex,' Red butted in, 'you can imagine anything. You'll find that out soon enough.'

'It's that bad, eh?'

'It's that bad.'

'I'm having nightmares already.'

Saying no more, the three men sat there and waited for the helicopter to arrive from Vung Tau with the replacements. While they were waiting, Dead-eye returned from the edge of the paddy-field, clearly visible now that the smoke had cleared, and reported that there were no more VC between the hide and the edge of the jungle.

'Did you go into the jungle itself?' Shagger asked him.

'Yes. Just a few hundred yards. Far enough to hear the sounds of battle about a mile farther on.'

'Shouldn't take long to get to them,' Red said.

'It might take a lot longer than you expect,' Dead-eye told him. 'It turns into secondary jungle about a hundred yards in – and that's going to be hell to get through.'

Dead-eye was right, for land once cleared, then not used and allowed to revert to its original state, grows back even thicker and more tangled than it was before. Ahead of them was a dense sea of thorn, bracken, bamboo and tall grass with sharp blades.

Minutes later a USAF CH-47 Chinook helicopter appeared in the afternoon's grey sky, coming from the direction of Vung Tau. As it dropped vertically, its twin rotors created a whirlwind that sucked up water, pebbles and foliage, but its large, low-pressure tyres enabled it to land in the paddy-field without sinking into it. The ramp in the rear of its watertight fuselage was already open when it landed, so even before the rotors had stopped spinning, two-man teams bearing stretchers between them hurried out to pick up the dead VC soldiers. As they were rolling the bullet-riddled, bloody bodies on to stretchers, to be flown in the Chinook to a mass burial ground near Vung Tau, more members of the Australian 5th Battalion poured out, all heavily armed and humping pallets filled with equipment, to take up positions around the VC hide and begin the construction of what would be a long-term OP with defensive gun positions.

As the new arrivals toiled away, the Chinook roared back into life, its rotors whipping up another whirlwind that battered at them viciously. The helicopter ascended vertically, hovered about fifty feet above the ground, then headed back towards Vung Tau.

'Let's go and join Team 2,' Shagger said, 'and check out those bunkers.'

The four men wearily picked themselves up, splashed through the last fifty yards of the paddy-field, and entered the jungle in single file, then merged with the shadows and disappeared.

9

The first hundred yards or so were relatively easy, with the ground firm underfoot, the temperature lower because of the lack of sunlight, the foliage fairly light and the trees spaced well apart. Though still advancing at the crouch, weapons at the ready, and keeping their eyes peeled for booby-traps, the men were able to zigzag their way forward with little trouble.

But then, as Dead-eye had warned them, they came abruptly into secondary jungle, where the trees were much closer together and the undergrowth was an impenetrable tangle of thorny branches, gigantic, razor-sharp palm leaves, interwoven rattan, tall grass with vicious edges, and densely packed bamboo. Much of the overhanging foliage was covered in cobwebs that contained poisonous spiders and, as the men were uneasily aware, various kind of snake – some venomous, others not – were inclined to sleep curled around the branches and looked very much like them.

They could now hear the sounds of battle from up ahead, where the advance of Team 2 had been blocked by the VC bunker complex. That mile, they feared, would take several hours to traverse.

'We don't have any choice,' Dead-eye said. 'We'll have to hack our way through with the machetes, and look out for booby-traps at the same time, so it won't be easy.'

'One man at a time,' Shagger suggested. 'One man takes the lead and cuts his way through with his machete while the others follow, giving him cover should the need arise. We all take turns with the machete, fifteen minutes each. I don't think any of us could stick it for longer than that at one stretch. What do you think?'

Dead-eye and Jimbo nodded.

'I agree,' Red said.

'Since it's my bright idea,' Shagger said generously, 'I'll be the first to go out front.'

'Good on you,' Red said sardonically.

Shagger slung his assault rifle over his shoulder then untied the machete from his belt. Without another word, he stepped out ahead of the others and began hacking his way through the dense, tangled undergrowth. The other men fell back into single file behind him, spaced well apart, scanning the jungle to the front and both sides. As Tail-end Charlie, Jimbo also had to turn round repeatedly to cover their rear, though he knew it was unlikely that any VC would now come from that direction.

Progress was painfully slow. After chopping through the undergrowth with his machete, Shagger often had to tear the shredded foliage away with his bare hands, or push it to the side, in order to create a passage. Each blow of the machete would cause dust to rise in clouds from the branches and leaves, which would themselves shake violently, causing gigantic, sharp-edged palm leaves to whip into Shagger's face. Within minutes he was dripping with sweat, covered in bloody scratches, and being attacked by frenzied mosquitoes and midges. What slowed him down even more were the spiders and other insects that frequently fell on to him from the overhanging branches, making him stop to frantically slap them off his head, shoulders and arms. By the end of his first fifteen minutes he was exhausted and gratefully swapped places with Dead-eye.

Though one of the toughest men in 22 SAS, Dead-eye, like Shagger, was exhausted and soaked in his own sweat by the time his stint was over. He then swapped places with Red, who endured his quarter of an hour of hell, then swapped places with Jimbo. Fifteen minutes later, at the end of the first hour, it was Shagger's turn again. By that time they had only managed to cover less than a quarter of a mile.

As Shagger unslung the SLR from his shoulder and prepared to attack the undergrowth once again, Jimbo nodded back over his shoulder.

'The gunfire certainly seems a lot closer,' he said, trying to sound as encouraging as he could.

'Bloody oath,' Shagger replied, then started hacking furiously with the machete as Jimbo headed back to the end of the line.

Again, Shagger had to suffer the hell of sweat, choking dust, noisy, bloodthirsty insects, rebounding branches and spiders and other creepy-crawlies dropping on to his head, shoulders and arms. Once he sprang back instinctively, cursing, when a startled snake hissed at him. He steadied himself, then lunged and chopped off its head. When the two pieces of the snake had fallen off the branch to the ground, he watched in amazement as the tongue of the severed head kept darting in and out and the rest of the body wriggled into the undergrowth, leaving a trail of blood and only stopping when the blood had drained out of it completely.

Shuddering, Shagger went back to work, slashing his way forward for another five minutes, until he stopped suddenly by a warning cry from Dead-eye.

'Freeze!'

Shagger froze like a statue in the act of swinging the machete, and remained in that pose for several seconds, hardly breathing, sweat pouring down his face, before finally croaking: 'What . . .?'

'Don't move anything but your head,' Dead-eye told him. 'Look down at your feet. Can you see something stretched across the ground, about ankle level?'

Shagger glanced gingerly down at the ground. 'No. Nothing. Just the undergrowth . . . No! There's something there. It looks like a camouflaged trip cord.'

'Is your leg touching it?'

'No. It's a couple of inches away from my shin, just above the ankle.'

'Anything at waist level?'

Shagger raised his gaze slightly, squinting into the foliage he had just been about to attack. 'Shit! A bow-shaped length of bamboo at waist level and covered in foliage. I can only see part of it.'

'OK,' Dead-eye said. 'Step away from it – slowly. Try not to shake anything. Take a couple of steps back, check that there's no trip cord right or left, then get well to the side of the area you've been trying to clear. Move very carefully now.'

Shagger blinked the sweat from his eyes, lowered the machete to his side, then very carefully took a couple of steps backward. When he was well away from the trip cord, he checked left and right, saw nothing, and stepped cautiously to his right. Without being told, Red and Jimbo did the same, taking up positions on either side of the passage hacked out by their team-mate. Finally Dead-eye did the same, positioning himself behind a tree and aiming down at the trip cord with his SLR. He switched to automatic and fired a sustained burst that sent leaves and soil leaping wildly in the air before tearing the trip cord to shreds.

Instantly, the length of bamboo was released and whipped forward with tremendous force, smashing noisily through the undergrowth and quivering like a bowstring when it reached its limit, with its vicious, razor-sharp spikes forming a line across the route at body level.

Those spikes would have impaled anyone in their path, leading to an excruciating death.

'Shit!' Jimbo whispered.

'Right through your cock and nuts,' Red said with a sly grin. 'You'd be singing a couple of octaves higher – and maybe sweating a little . . . Before bleeding to death, of course.'

'I've got to hand it to you,' Shagger said to Dead-eye. 'You've got the eyes of a hawk.'

'It's easier to see when you're not in the thick of it, swinging that machete.' Dead-eye raised his hand and studied his watch, then said dispassionately, 'You've still got five minutes to go, so get back to work, Sarge.'

'Fair enough,' Shagger said with a sigh, and then stepped carefully around the spiked length of bamboo and resumed his task as the others fell into single file behind him.

As the team's slow, back-breaking work continued, the outbreaks of gunfire from up ahead became louder, letting them know that they were at least making progress. Each of the four-man team had another stint of fifteen minutes with the machete, which took another hour and carried them beyond the half mile mark, or approximately halfway.

119

Another reason why the going was so slow was that they had to stop frequently, either to enable chopped undergrowth to be dragged aside by hand or because of more booby-traps, including an angled-arrow trap. When Dead-eye had tripped the cord by blasting it apart with his SLR, the trap fired a steel arrow from a length of bamboo fixed to a piece of board covered with foliage. It was a deadly device.

Eventually, when they had covered about three-quarters of a mile, the secondary jungle gave way to normal jungle and the machete was no longer needed.

'Thank Christ for that,' Red whispered, wiping sweat from his forehead.

'Bit exhausting for you, was it?' Jimbo asked him.

'Bloody oath, mate.'

'Can you see *me* sweating?' Jimbo said, having already wiped his face dry with a cloth when Red wasn't looking. 'It's all down to good training.'

'Stop kidding yourself, mate. I can tell you're shagged by the sound of your breathing. I bet that handkerchief in your pocket's soaked with sweat. You must take me for a right fucking dill. Pah! Your training's no tougher than ours.'

Jimbo grinned and was about to retort when Shagger, who had been listening intently to the gunfire, turned back to them and used a hand signal to indicate that they should resume single file and press on. This they did, with Dead-eye again out on point and Jimbo bringing up the rear. The going was now much easier, though they still had to contend with the humidity, attacking insects and poisonous snakes, as well as remaining alert to the threat of mines or booby-traps.

After another half hour the noise of light machine-guns and AK47s was much louder, almost directly ahead, and being answered by Team 2's SLRs and single GPMG.

Even as they were advancing that last hundred yards, there was a particularly loud explosion, followed by a fountain of soil, uprooted foliage, leaves and billowing smoke.

'That was an 85mm missile,' Shagger said as he came up to stand beside Dead-eye, with the other two bunched up just behind them. 'Fired from a VC grenade launcher. Probably an RPG7V. Let's make sure we put *that* fucker out of action. Come on, cobbers, let's pick it up.'

The debris had stopped raining down and the smoke was drifting lazily when Shagger broke into a trot and the others followed suit, spreading out as they advanced and flitting from one tree to the other to avoid sniper fire. A few minutes later they arrived at what appeared to be a dried river-bed or gully, which Team 2 had taken over as a natural defensive position. The four of them were down there now. Just below the lip of the rise, Corporals Bob 'Blue' Butler and Michael 'Mad Mike' Dalton were manning the 7.72mm M60 GPMG, the former firing, the latter feeding the belt in. Sergeant Don Ingrams was kneeling beside the radio, bawling into the receiver while covering his left ear with his other hand to keep out the roaring of the guns. Beside him, but lying on his belly, Sergeant Giles Norton was methodically firing his combination 5.56mm M16A1 automatic rifle and M203 grenade launcher.

As Shagger and the others slid down into the river-bed, Norton fired a high-explosive round from his own M203. Dead-eye had already clambered up the other side of the gully and was peering over its lip when the round exploded with a harsh, bellowing sound, blowing enormous chunks of concrete off the bunker in the undergrowth two hundred yards away. When the smoke cleared, the bunker was still there, though great chunks of one corner had been blown off. It was a rectangular bunker with slit windows, through which the barrels of a machine-gun and other automatic weapons were poking out.

As if in retaliation for the grenade, the VC guns in the slit windows opened fire, turning the lip of the river-bed into a storm of spitting sand and flying stones which showered down on the men positioned on the slope.

'Shit!' Ingrams growled, wiping dirt from his eyes as he turned to face Shagger and Dead-eye. 'Good to see you, cobber.'

'You look knackered.'

'I am. We *all* are. Those bastards are well dug in and they're heavily armed.'

'You can stop shitting your pants now, mate,' Shagger said. 'We're here to give you support.'

'You won't be enough, but you'll do for now. I think we've got a whole regiment of VC out there, some in bunkers, others sniping at us from the jungle and constantly changing position. I've called for a couple of gunships to blow them to buggery, though we have to keep them occupied till the choppers get here. The airfield and village are a mile beyond that bunker complex, so no question: they have to be cleared. It's a fucking tough nut, though.'

'It won't break our teeth,' Shagger replied.

'Then let's do it,' Dead-eye said. 'How much space are they occupying over there?'

Ingrams indicated east and west with his left hand. 'The bunkers are spaced out to cover a front of about two hundred yards. Six bunkers evenly spread, but with more behind them, hidden by the trees. They also have what seems to be the rest of the regiment scattered through the trees, forming a protective cordon around the bunkers. Those bastards are the ones keeping us pinned down. They're the reason we can't encircle the bunkers. We have to remove them first.'

'No,' Shagger said. 'We have to deal with the bunkers first.' He checked his map, then looked up again. 'We'll call in Teams 5 and 9,' he said. 'They're patrolling right along this perimeter. They could all be here in thirty minutes, or an hour at most, to make up our strength. By that time the gunships should have been here to blow those bunkers to hell. When they've done that, our four teams combined can shoot their way through the complex, mopping up as we go.'

'That sounds rough to me,' Ingrams said.

'Bloody oath, it'll be rough,' Shagger replied, 'but it's all we can do. We have to take this place over by last light, then rest up and attack the village tomorrow. There's no other way.'

Shagger then called out to Red, 'Get on that radio and contact Teams 5 and 9. Give them this location and tell them to get here immediately. Remind them about the booby-traps and mines, but apart from those they're to make no detours. Tell them they were wanted here yesterday.'

'No problem, Sarge,' Red replied. 'Yesterday it is.'

'Bloody oath,' Shagger said. As Red fiddled with the radio, Shagger turned to Ingrams and asked, 'When you called up the gunships, did you . . .?'

He was cut short when the GPMG operated by Blue and Mad Mike roared into action, sending a stream of purple tracer in a phosphorescent arc that sent bullets ricocheting off the partially concealed concrete bunkers. The tracer moved left and right to hit one bunker after the other, filling the air around them with flying pieces of concrete and cement and choking dust. The instant the GPMG fell silent, as Mad Mike was feeding in another belt of ammunition, the VC in the bunkers responded in kind, tearing the lip of the river-bed apart with a sustained, deafening burst from the RPD light machine-gun. This burst of fire was followed almost instantly by the muffled thudding sound of their grenade launcher. The missile exploded with a savage roaring near the gully, filling the air with boiling smoke and showering the men with soil and foliage.

'Bloody hell!' Shagger yelled, ducking low and shielding his eyes. He remained that way until the RPD had stopped firing, then straightened up again and continued the conversation he'd been having before with Ingrams. 'When you called up the gunships, did you also call up for replacements to take over that bunker complex?'

'Well, no, I . . .'

'Red! Shagger snapped, turning to his trustworthy signaller. 'When you've finished with Teams 5 and 9, tell HQ we need a replacement detail – at least fifty men – to take over this bunker complex and hold it as a defensive position. We'll also need some APCs and a couple of Centurions. Got that?'

Red, who had earphones on and was speaking into the receiver, gave the thumbs up to indicate that he had understood the message to HQ.

'So,' Shagger said, turning to Dead-eye and Jimbo. 'Now we wait.'

'Can I smoke?' Jimbo asked.

'As Charlie obviously knows where we are, I don't see why not. Light up, cobber!'

Dead-eye didn't smoke, but Shagger, Jimbo and Red lit up and inhaled with pleasure as they awaited the arrival of the helicopter gunships. Sergeant Norton fired another missile from his combination 5.56mm M16A1 automatic rifle and M203 grenade launcher, then slid back down to the river-bed to enjoy a smoke with the others.

'Waste of my bloody time,' he told them. 'Might as well relax.' The GPMG roared into action above them, still being fired by Blue and Mad Mike. 'They fire at anything that moves,' Norton added, exhaling a thin stream of cigarette smoke. 'A pair of real enthusiasts.'

About thirty minutes later four helicopters appeared in the sky, coming from the direction of Vung Tau. Gradually they became recognizable as Cobra gunships armed with heavy machine-guns and rockets. Crawling back up to the lip of the gully, Shagger studied the VC bunkers, then guided the Cobra in with his SARBE. After clambering up beside him, Norton used his grenade launcher to drop a couple of coloured smoke bombs on to the enemy bunkers, clearly marking the target.

The VC had seen the helicopters as well and began firing from the bunkers with machine-guns and assault weapons. Ignoring this fusillade, the choppers descended one by one to attack the bunkers with simultaneous bursts of heavy machine-gun fire and rockets. The results were both spectacular and fearsome, with hundreds of bullets ricocheting noisily off the bunkers and the rockets exploding in silvery-yellow flames licking through vast clouds of black, oily smoke. The darting fingers of flame then set fire to the trees and turned the jungle immediately around the bunkers into an inferno.

As the trees blazed, black-shirted VC could be discerned running frantically to and fro, some of them on fire and screaming hideously. Instantly, the SAS in the river-bed opened fire with their personal weapons and two GPMGs, picking off the guerrillas in the burning, smoking jungle.

Pinned down by the awesome might of the four Cobra gunships, the VC in the bunkers had stopped firing and could do little to retaliate as their positions were riddled by repeated bursts of heavy machine-gun fire, then systematically blown apart and scorched by the exploding rockets.

As this was going on, the eight men of Teams 5 and 9 emerged from the jungle behind and slipped down into the gully beside the others, their weapons clattering noisily as they settled in.

'Jesus!' Team 5's Sergeant Bloomfield said, glancing over the lip of the river-bed to where the bunkers were being blown apart by the gunships' rockets. 'That's some pounding they're getting.'

'They won't stop until all those bunkers have been smashed to hell,' Shagger informed him. 'That's the whole point.'

'Then we advance on the VC in the jungle?'

'You've hit the nail on the head, mate.'

By this time the four Cobras were hovering over the bunker complex, all firing their rockets and heavy machine-guns simultaneously, turning the area into a hell of flying concrete, pluming smoke, spiralling dust and blazing foliage. Behind and around the bunkers, the VC not in the bunkers were either running from the flames or firing up at the helicopters in futile gestures of defiance. Thus exposed, they were cut down by the SAS men in the gully, who picked them off with a combination of GPMGs and personal weapons.

The clash lasted for some twenty minutes, although it seemed much longer to all involved. When the Cobras ascended to return to Vung Tau, the remains of the bunkers could scarcely be discerned through dense clouds of smoke and dust. Some of the trees in the surrounding jungle were still burning, though most were charred and smouldering.

'Right,' Shagger said to the three PCs grouped around him, 'tell your men to move out and advance on the bunkers and the jungle surrounding them. Teams 1 and 2 will advance directly on the bunkers and clean them up. Team 5 will go round the left side of the bunker and advance into the jungle.

Team 9 will do the same on the right side of the bunker. When Teams 1 and 2 have finished off those still alive in the bunker, they'll advance into the jungle. By that time the 6th Battalion replacements should have arrived to turn what's left of the bunker complex into one of our own defensive positions. OK, let's move out.'

When Shagger's instructions had been relayed to the rest of the men along the gully, they all clambered up the sloping side and began their cautious advance.

Immediately, sporadic rifle fire came from the jungle on both sides of the bunkers, though none from the bunkers themselves. The SAS men ran from the cover of one tree to another, though they broke up into three separate teams, with two four-man teams, 5 and 9, moving around the side of the bunkers towards the burning jungle beyond and an eight-man team, composed of Teams 1 and 2, advancing right into the bunker complex. Once in the scorched, shattered remains of the sunken bunkers they were partially protected from sniper fire, though they had to make their way through the appalling tangle of scorched and broken bodies. Few of the VC were still alive and those few were in a bad way, scarcely able to move. In fact, there was not one man in the bunker in a condition to resist.

There was no threat left here, though the gunshots from the jungle on both sides of the bunker indicated that Teams 5 and 9 were engaging the enemy.

Even as the combined teams were examining the last of the bunkers, two USAF Chinooks from Nui Dat roared in over the complex, whipping up dust and the smoke from the smouldering trees. Guided in by a coloured smoke bomb put down by Jimbo, the helicopters settled on a path of cleared ground between the trees and the bunkers. The rear ramps were already down and while the rotors were still turning heavily armed soldiers of D Company, 6th Battalion RAR/ NZ hurried out and swarmed all over the bunker complex. The burial detail had already started collecting up the hideously burnt and broken VC dead for mass burial and the medics were carrying the VC wounded into the Chinooks as Shagger led Teams 1 and 2 away from the complex and into the jungle. There the other SAS men were engaged in close quarter battle (CQB) with the guerrillas who had survived the burning trees.

The fires had mostly gone out, but the trees were still smouldering and the jungle was filled with blinding, choking smoke. The CQB therefore became a cat-and-mouse game, with the SAS men advancing at the crouch, darting from one tree to the next, straining to see through the smoke, and firing at the black-shirted figures who suddenly leaned out from behind tree trunks or popped up from behind tangled undergrowth to fire their AK47s. It was like being in the Killing House in Hereford, except that the figures abruptly materializing in the smoke were not cardboard cut-outs with painted weapons, but flesh-and-blood men intent on revenge for the attack.

Realizing that the jungle was still thick with VC, the SAS men formed two-man teams, with one man giving covering fire to the other as he advanced, and vice versa. In this way they managed to advance slowly, and did so without taking any casualties.

Gradually they were reinforced by men from D Company, 6th Battalion, until nearly a hundred Australian and New Zealand troops were engaged in the CQB to clear the jungle that surrounded the bunkers and also led to the edge of the village that was to be their target the next day.

Four of them were killed and nearly a dozen were wounded before the last of the VC called it a day and came out from their hides with their hands raised. After being disarmed, they were blindfolded with 'sweat rags', bound with toggle ropes, and then marched at gunpoint back to the Chinooks, to be flown to the POW cage at Nui Dat.

By last light, when the trees had finally stopped smouldering and the smoke had cleared, the battle for the bunker complex had ended and the way was clear to make the assault on the VC-held airfield and village.

10

The light had gone completely when the Chinooks which had taken the wounded Aussies and VC back to Vung Tau returned one after another to offload more equipment and vehicles, including six armoured personnel carriers and two fifty-ton Centurion Mark V tanks, which would be used in the next day's advance against the VC stronghold. They also dropped the two bulldozers requested for the digging of a mass grave for the VC dead, which would be done by simply shovelling up the soil and corpses together, pushing them into a great hole, and covering that hole up with earth. The bulldozers were already doing this when a second wave of Chinooks arrived with more men and equipment.

The helicopters came down on an LZ located close to the devastated bunker complex and illuminated with crude petrol flares. Whipped up by the spinning rotors, the dust swirled violently across the lights and bathed the men waiting below in a flickering, strobe-like effect that made everyone feel unreal and disorientated. The helicopters kept coming and going until midnight, by which time the area was a hive of activity and the VC bunker complex was already well on the way to becoming a fortified defensive position for the Australians.

Lieutenant-Colonel Callaghan was one of those who walked down the ramp at the rear of the last Chinook. Crossing from the LZ to what had once been the VC stronghold, he was gratified to see that the construction of a circular FOB was already well under way, with one bulldozer interring a pile of VC corpses, a second clearing and flattening the ground for the eventual erection of tents to be used as headquarters, stores, armoury, communications, mess and a parking area for the APCs and tanks. Many of the other troops were already constructing sangars, placed equidistant in a circle to form a defensive ring around the camp. Eventually the sangars would become hedgehogs, bristling with machine-guns and other heavy weapons.

No one led Callaghan to the site selected for the HQ tent, but he recognized it instantly by the ranks of those gathered around it. Joining that group, he was introduced to Lieutenant-Colonel Ronald Fallow, CO of the replacement troops who would take over this captured site. After shaking hands, the two men cracked a couple of cans of beer and sat on wooden packing crates, facing each other over a third crate serving as a table. All around them, work on the construction of the camp was continuing in the pale light of the moon, under a vast, starry sky.

'A busy little place,' Callaghan said, nodding to indicate the many men still noisily working or raising pup tents in the moonlit darkness about him.

'Hard yacker,' Fallow said, meaning hard work, 'but they'll get it done on time.'

'By first light tomorrow.'

'Too right, Paddy. So here's to the mission.' They tapped their beer cans together then drank.

'You think you can hold this position?' Callaghan asked, lowering his can of beer.

'It's contained and will remain that way,' Fallow replied with confidence. 'Besides, all the VC have been cleared out from the base camp to here, so the only ones left are directly ahead, between here and the village. This camp won't be under threat of attack and we can only go one way – forward.'

'It promises to be one hell of a fight.'

'It will be,' Fallow said. 'But the SAS are going in first, so they'll take the brunt of it. A rough ride, I fear.'

'They'll manage,' Callaghan said.

'They're clearing the way for 5 and 6 Battalions?'

'Correct. Their job is to check for minefields, booby-traps and VC OPs or ambush positions and, if found, remove them. We'll be in constant touch with both battalions by radio and guide them in to the village.'

'Sounds sweet,' Fallow said. 'But there's an airfield by the village – that has to be taken care of first. And there's also a VC tunnel system right under the village.'

'I know. That's the last job to be done.'

'Hell on earth – or *under* the earth, to be more precise. Are you sending your men down?'

'Yes,' Callaghan said. 'My *only* two men.'

'They're going to have to be better than good,' Fallow told him, sounding grim. 'Those tunnel systems are a bloody nightmare.'

'So we've been told.'

'Have they ever been in a tunnel system before?'

'No, but they're going down with some experienced Aussie tunnel rats.'

'Shagger and Red.'

'That's the two.'

'Good men. You won't find much better.'

'So how are my two men getting on with the Aussies?' Callaghan asked.

'No problems that I know of, but you better ask them. Given the nature of Australians, there's bound to be a fair bit of bull, but I'm sure your men can give as good as they get.'

'We call it "bullshit", not "bull", and we can certainly dish it out.'

Fallow chuckled. 'I'll bet.' He drank some more beer, wiped his lips with the back of his hand, then glanced about him at the men working by moonlight and the eerie glow of spotlights as helicopters ascended and descended in billowing clouds of dust.

By now, just outside the main compound, the bloody, mangled VC dead had been bulldozed into an immense ditch and covered in soil and vegetation. Inside the compound, large and small tents had been erected. Stacks of wooden packing crates were being opened and their contents moved into the relevant tents. Where the ground had been flattened by bulldozers and men with hoes, 5th and 6th Battalion troops were digging shallow scrapes and defensive trenches or raising pup tents to be used as accommodation. In the stone-walled sangars, heavy machine-guns and twenty-five-pounders were being placed in position. The whole place was frantic.

'Impressive,' Callaghan said, suddenly filling up with a sense of loss, for this was almost certainly the last time he would serve overseas.

'Aussies work and play hard,' Fallow said. 'They've already got a bar over there, complete with jukebox, and the open-air movies will be running by tomorrow night. If they could open a brothel, they would, but they'll make do. And no matter how hung over they are tomorrow morning, they'll move out and fight like nobody's business. That's the Aussie way.'

'We Brits are a little more modest, but we're not far behind you.'

Fallow grinned and raised his glass in the air in a mocking toast. 'Better go and have a chat with your two men, so they won't feel so lonely. You'll find them in one of those pup tents, having their last night of rest. Early rise tomorrow.'

'For everyone,' Callaghan reminded him.

'That's the picture, Paddy.'

'Thanks,' Callaghan said. He finished off his beer, dropped the can into the rubbish bin beside Fallow's makeshift table, then stood up and walked across the compound to the row of tents. He had to be careful where he walked because the ground was now littered with opened crates, weapons, medical equipment, petrol cans, and boxes of food and drink, with men busily unpacking them and relaying their contents to the relevant tents. At the same time, helicopters continued to ascend and descend, making a hell of a din and whipping up the dust, while the Centurions and APCs were being tested, which added to the bedlam.

Eventually managing to wend his way through what appeared to be organized chaos, he reached the pup tents and followed the line until he came to two SAS-constructed lean-tos which were facing away from the wind. Dead-eye and Jimbo were in those, sitting side by side and checking their weapons.

'I don't think you'll need that Browning tomorrow,' Callaghan said. 'It'll be a straightforward rifle job.'

Both men glanced up, surprised to see their CO. They were sitting on their hollow-fill sleeping-bags, beside a rudimentary portable kitchen consisting of a hexamine stove, an aluminium mess tin, mugs and utensils; and a brew kit, including sachets of tea, powdered milk and sugar. Spread out on a rubber groundsheet were spare radio batteries, water bottles, extra ammunition, matches and flint; an emergency first-aid kit, signal flares, and various survival aids, such as compass, pencil torch and batteries; even surgical blades and butterfly sutures. Dead-eye smiled slightly, but Jimbo grinned in his customary broad, cocky manner.

'You know us, boss,' Jimbo said. 'Always prepared for any eventuality. Just doing our daily cleaning and check as we were taught back in Hereford.'

'I'm glad to see it,' Callaghan replied, kneeling on the ground between the two men. 'So where are your two Aussie mates?'

Dead-eye jerked his thumb toward a brightly lit tent from which rock 'n' roll was blaring. 'In the bar, having a few pints.'

'I'm surprised you're not with them. Loosen up a bit. Relax.'

'We will do,' Jimbo assured him, 'when these weapons are cleaned. So what's brought you here, boss?'

Callaghan shrugged. 'Just a visit. I wanted to see for myself what's happening here, and I must say it looks pretty impressive.'

'These Aussies know what they're doing,' Dead-eye said. 'You've got to hand it to them.'

'So how are you getting on with them? Any problems?'

'Nope,' Jimbo said. 'They tend to be pretty sharp with their tongues, but otherwise they're OK. They don't seem to resent us any more and we get on just fine. I think we still have to prove ourselves in certain ways, but so far they seem pleased with us.'

'Good,' Callaghan said. 'What about Shagger and Red in particular? Do you get on with them?'

'Yes,' Jimbo said. 'They're no different from the others. They treat us the same way. They keep slinging the bullshit, but they get as good as they give and they're gradually coming round to accepting us as part of the team.'

'They'll be with you when you attack the airfield and village tomorrow?'

'Yep. Them and some other Aussie SAS teams.'

'Four-man patrols?'

'Mainly, though in certain situations we double up the teams for greater strike force.'

'But generally you're passing muster with them?' Callaghan asked.

'Generally speaking, yes.'

'The real test's still to come,' Dead-eye said. 'Down in the tunnel complex. Shagger and Red are really proud of their capabilities down there and are challenging us with it. If we go down there, and if we come up again in one piece, then we'll have won their respect.'

'And mine,' Callaghan said. He glanced around the busy base camp with what seemed like sadness.

'What are you thinking, boss?' Dead-eye asked him.

Callaghan sighed. 'My last active tour of duty, Dead-eye. After this, it's back to a boring desk job. Time certainly moves on.'

'You'll really miss it.'

'Yes.'

'You're not alone,' Jimbo said. 'My own time's running out and the next stop is the Training Wing. That isn't exactly a desk job, but it isn't active service either. It's the first step on the road to retirement and I can't bear to think about it.'

'You always were a bantam cock,' Callaghan told him. 'From the very earliest days in North Africa. You've been through a lot, Jimbo.'

'You survived even more, boss,' Jimbo replied. 'A legend in your own time.'

Callaghan flushed slightly. 'Now, now,' he said. 'Hopefully I'm old enough not to let that go to my head. But thanks for the thought.'

Then his face took on once more that distracted, rather sad look as he cast his gaze towards the LZs. There, two Chinook helicopters were competing to see which could make the most noise and most dramatic dust storm as they descended side by side on to their respective landing pads. When they had touched down and were disgorging more troops, who emerged ghostlike from the billowing dust, Callaghan sighed again involuntarily, then picked up a fistful of dry soil and let it fall in a thin stream through his fingers.

'Oh, well,' he said softly.

Embarrassed himself now, Jimbo cleared his throat, then asked, 'Are you giving a briefing?'

'No. Lieutenant-Colonel Fallow is. At first light. The rest of the evening is free, gentlemen, so why not go and join the others? Enjoy yourselves.'

'Might just do that,' Jimbo said, completing the oiling of his SLR, which he slung over his shoulder just before Dead-eye did the same. 'Come on, Dead-eye, let's go.'

The three men stood together and Callaghan patted the shoulders of his two sergeants. 'Good luck,' he said, then walked off in the direction of Fallow's large tent, his spine as straight as a ramroad.

'The last of the best,' Dead-eye said.

'You're right,' Jimbo replied. 'Come on, let's go and get pissed.'

They crossed the compound to where the rock 'n' roll was pounding out from one of the larger tents. Stepping inside, they found the makeshift pub absolutely packed, with men sitting shoulder to shoulder on planks laid over beer barrels, resting elbows over beer glasses on other planks being used as tables. The jukebox was a flashing, brightly coloured Wurlitzer purchased from the Yanks. Smoke from numerous cigarettes filled the air and the conversation was loud.

Shagger and Red were sitting side by side on one of the benches, both ruddy and fairly drunk. Having earlier invited Dead-eye and Jimbo over for a drink, they had kept two spaces available on the bench directly facing them over the barrel-top table.

'It's the Poms!' Red said with a big grin, then indicated the places opposite him and Shagger. 'Have a seat, cobbers, and I'll fill up your glasses.'

When Dead-eye and Jimbo had squeezed themselves in, Shagger poured them a schooner of beer each from one of the many six-pint jugs on the table, then they all raised their glasses in a mock toast.

'To our poncey Pommy mates!' Shagger exclaimed.

'To our grog-happy Aussie no-hopers playing silly buggers,' Jimbo shot back.

Shagger laughed. 'Learning the language, I see,' he said. 'You'll soon be able to emigrate and communicate with the natives.'

'I haven't been given my ball and chain yet,' Jimbo replied.

'Convicts are men of initiative who just got caught,' Red informed him. 'The criminal classes produce the real survivors, which is why we Aussies, with our ball-and-chain roots, are the bastards you just can't beat.'

'Bastards with big heads,' Dead-eye said. 'That's about as far as it goes, mate.'

'That's about as far as your sense of humour goes, more like,' said Shagger.

Dead-eye gave a wan smile. 'I've never seen much to joke about,' he said. 'It just doesn't come naturally, that's all.'

'I told you Dead-eye had seen some things in Malaya. You're not the same after experiences like that,' said Jimbo, anxious to defend his mate.

'So what happened there, cobber?' Red asked Dead-eye, who cast an angry glance at Jimbo and said in a monotone, 'Not much. Just the usual shit. I wouldn't . . .'

'Bullshit,' Jimbo interrupted. 'Sorry, Dead-eye. It must have been a fucking nightmare. Men spiked on punji stakes, crushed under spiked logs, heads chopped off with *parangs*, dead bodies floating in the swamps. Then on top of that, snakes, leeches, poisonous insects, vicious wild oxen and ravenous mosquitoes. And Dead-eye saw it all.'

'That's enough, Jimbo,' growled Dead-eye.

But Jimbo ignored his mate's plea and continued. 'In one instance, one of the men fell into a pit of punji stakes smeared with human shit as well as poison and had to be pulled off the fuckers. It was a nightmare . . .'

'Jimbo!' Dead-eye said threateningly.

'Another time,' Jimbo went on, oblivious, 'one of Dead-eye's best friends, Ralph Lorrimer, had his head chopped off by a commie bitch with a *parang*. Then, when his head fell on the ground, propped up on the severed neck and pumping blood, the eyes kept darting left and right, as if the poor bastard was desperately wondering what had happened to him. Dead-eye was there when it happened, which is why we nicknamed him . . .'

Very quietly, with wonderful economy of movement, Dead-eye leant sideways, grabbed the collar of Jimbo's tunic in his right fist and hauled him forward until they were eyeball to eyeball.

'I said that's enough!' Dead-eye whispered, his face icy with suppressed rage. 'And I mean it. I don't want to be reminded of that business, so let's change the subject.'

Choking, hardly able to speak, but brutally reminded that Dead-eye had always refused to discuss the horrors of the

Telok Anson swamp, Jimbo just nodded frantically until his friend released him. 'Sorry, Dead-eye,' he said. 'Forgot myself. Just running off at the mouth there. The drink went to my head.'

'OK,' Dead-eye said. He raised his glass to his lips, drained the remaining beer in one gulp, filled the glass again and then took another long pull at it. 'No problem.'

'What I want,' Red said, to calm the mood, 'is one night with my sheila.'

'Nice, is she?' Jimbo asked.

'Tits like cantaloups and built like a brick shithouse, that's my Mildred,' Red informed him.

'It's true love,' Shagger said. 'You can tell by the way he talks about her. Real romantic, Red is.'

'I was born in North Queensland,' Red explained. 'Not too much choice up there. You found someone who dropped her frilly knickers for you and you thought you were made. You put it in, you pulled it out, you wiped it dry and then you went to the altar and slipped on the gold ring. Jugs like cantaloups went a long way back home and they still do it for me.'

'The man's a poet,' Shagger said, trying to keep a straight face.

'I give her what she needs,' Red insisted, failing to see the joke. 'The old in-and-out. Two kids and another in the oven. And regular money. What more could a woman want?'

'You Aussies are so sensitive,' Jimbo said, 'I could cry in my beer.'

'I like a woman in her place,' Red informed him, 'which is flat on her back. What about you, Dead-eye?'

The question was not as casual as it sounded. In fact, Shagger and Red were both impressed by Dead-eye's calm,

141

impassive nature and intrigued over what had made him that way. The truth was that Dead-eye had lost so many SAS friends in hideous circumstances that he no longer wanted the pain of any emotional involvement. The traumas he had suffering in and after the horrors of Telok Anson had scarred him for good, and in the end broke up his marriage. Dead-eye did not like to show his feelings and sex could make a man do that. For that reason, he never became romantically involved with women – he only used them for sexual relief – and he had found that life was easier that way.

'I don't want to discuss my private life,' he told Red.

Dead-eye was a man wrapped in total privacy and dedicated to soldiering. He was a fighting machine, a stone-cold killer, and not a man to mess with. A good man to have on your side when the going got tough.

Red, who was admiring though a little scared of Dead-eye, merely nodded, slugged down some more beer, then glanced about him. 'Right,' he murmured. 'No sweat, mate.'

'What's happening tomorrow?' Dead-eye asked. 'Anybody know yet?'

'The briefing's at first light,' Shagger told him, 'but I've already got the gist of it from the CO. The basic plan is for softening-up airstrikes throughout the night, covering the area between here and the airfield and village. We, the Aussie SAS – welcome aboard, Poms – will then advance by foot on the airfield, clearing out any VC we find on the way and radioing back info on minefields, booby-traps, sniper positions and anything else of strategic importance. When we reach the airfield, we recce it and decide whether or not we can take it alone. If we can, we call up 5th and 6th Battalions, then attack the target ourselves, clearing the way for them to take it over. But if we think it's too strongly defended, we wait for the two battalions to arrive and lend us support. Once the airfield's been taken, we all advance together on the village. And once the village is taken, we secure the ground with the help of both battalions, then us four will descend into the tunnel complex beneath the village and try clearing it out.'

'Sounds like an exciting day,' Dead-eye said.

'Let's drink to it,' Shagger said.

Just as they were touching glasses, five minutes after midnight, a familiar bass throbbing was heard from outside. Nearly all of the men in the smoky, noisy tent glanced up, then some of them left their tables to see what was happening.

Shagger, Red, Dead-eye and Jimbo followed them, stepping out from under the folding flaps of the tent into the cooler, fresher air outside. Gazing up at the night sky, they saw an enormous white moon surrounded by stars. As the throbbing grew louder, the silhouette of a giant Stratofortress crossed the moon, then a second, a third, and more, until they were many, all surrounded by a fleet of helicopter gunships. They crossed the pale moon, passed under the sea of stars, filled the sky directly above the base camp, deafening the men with their combined roaring. Shadowing the clouds, they flew on to the VC-held territory south of the camp, with each plane or helicopter crossing the moon being replaced by another.

'Jesus Christ!' Red whispered, awed by the sheer number of bombers and helicopter gunships.

Within minutes, the first explosions illuminated the distant sky as jagged patches of white and yellow, followed by crimson tipped with blue, then dazzling silver and gold. They looked like abstract paintings, but were in fact the colours of hell, and the flames and smoke – which is what the beautiful colours represented – were followed almost instantly by the distant whining and bellowing of rocket fire and explosions.

Through the thickening smoke and multiplying colours, the silhouettes of the helicopters could be seen, ascending to low altitude, well below the Stratofortresses, to devastate the terrain with rockets and heavy machine-gun fire. Gradually, as if blood was seeping down out of the black, starry sky, the whole night took on a pale crimson hue streaked with yellow flames and billowing black smoke.

The bombers and gunships came and went, passing back and forth over the camp, engines roaring, jet engines whistling, props whipping up the air, making the clouds incandescent, blotting out whole swathes of stars, turning the night over the VC strongholds into spectacular webs of phosphorescent tracer, jagged sheets of flame, geysering sparks and tumbling smoke, until it looked as if the end of the world had come. It went on and on, for one hour, then two, and only at three in the morning did it finally cease. By then the land seemed to be on fire, with flames still flickering up in all directions as far as the eye could see, and the stars and the moon, which had formerly been so bright, obscured by the dense, drifting smoke.

Then, after what seemed like eternity, the last of the aircraft departed and a great silence descended.

'Four hours left for sleep,' Dead-eye said. 'I think we better get some.'

'Bloody oath!' Shagger agreed.

Slightly unsteady on their feet, the four men walked away from the still busy beer tent and then crawled into their separate lean-tos for a bit of shut-eye before the hell to come.

11

They left at first light, shortly after a hurried breakfast and the CO's briefing. Lieutenant-Colonel Fallow had told them little that they did not already know and most of them were glad when he finished and let them move out. Operating as a four-man advance party, Team 1 moved out an hour before 1 and 3 SAS.

The Englishmen were armed with 7.62mm L1A1 SLRs, the Aussies with 5.56mm M16A1 automatic rifles, and all four men had a 9mm L9A1 Browning semi-automatic pistol holstered on the hip, M26 high-explosive hand-grenades and ample spare ammunition.

As usual, Dead-eye was out on point, Shagger was second in line as PC, Red was behind him as signaller, heavily burdened with the radio, and Jimbo brought up the rear.

They were followed within minutes by Team 2, which had Ingrams as PC, with Blue and Mad Mike sharing the burden of the 7.62mm GPMG, and Norton, presently their Tail-end Charlie, armed with a combination 5.56mm M16A1 automatic rifle and M203 grenade launcher.

What they moved into, once they left the base camp, was a jungle landscape defoliated by the all-night air raids and bombardments from the twenty-five-pounders in Vung Tau. Normally the vegetation was a mixture of bamboo, head-high scrub and tall timber, but these had all been torn apart or scorched by the attacks and the blackened landscape was a scene of utter devastation.

At first the men advanced without trouble, using a standard operating procedure of ten minutes' movement, stop and listen for two or three minutes, ten minutes' movement, then finally a five-to-ten-minute break in all-round defence every hour. Eventually, however, as the temperature rose and the humidity increased, they approached the area devastated by the air raids and had to plough through swarms of fat, black flies that were buzzing noisily over the carcasses of the VC dead. These appeared to be as abundant as the flies, lying whole or in pieces – an arm here, a leg there, bloody intestines, exposed shattered bones – and were scattered broadly over the terrain, blending gruesomely into the charred and ravaged landscape.

It seemed inconceivable that anyone could have survived such carnage, but amazingly some had. The evidence was to be found in the many abandoned gun-pits and trenches, where boot prints were still visible in the scorched soil, heading south-east towards the airfield and village.

'You've got to admire them,' Dead-eye said, nodding at an abandoned gun-pit. 'Even in the middle of that hellish bombing and bombardment, they had the presence of mind to take everything with them. They didn't leave us a bloody thing.'

'They're tough little buggers, all right,' Red replied. 'They've all lived with this shit since childhood, practically being born and dying as soldiers. They've got nothing else, mate.'

'Let's keep moving,' Shagger said.

Now that they were in open, defoliated country, the two groups were advancing in the one, widely spread diamond formation, allowing optimum firepower to be focused on the front, though it left them more exposed in the smoky daylight. As they neared the airfield outside the village, after a two-mile hike, they came to the epicentre of the bombing raid and were forced to wend their way around enormous, charred bomb craters filled with human remains and destroyed ordnance. Yet even here, in this hideous devastation, the surviving VC had managed to booby-trap weapons, pieces of scorched, twisted equipment, and even the bodies of their dead comrades.

With Dead-eye up ahead, and the members of Team 2 covering both flanks, the men advanced at a snail's pace, stopping frequently to mark booby-traps for the sappers following to dismantle or defuse.

Amazingly, even before they reached the airfield, they were attacked by snipers who had survived the dreadful, night-long air raid. The first popped up from a camouflaged trapdoor in a shell hole filled with dead bodies. Not imagining for a second that even a VC could be fanatical enough to crawl back into that quagmire of scorched flesh and broken bones to dig himself a hide, the normally alert SAS men were caught completely off guard when the first short burst from a 7.62mm PPS43 sub-machine-gun shattered the silence.

Ingrams, out on the front of the left flank, took most of the burst. Shuddering violently, he was punched backwards and his rifle flew from his hands. Even as he was jerking epileptically on the ground amid spitting soil, dust and ash, those nearest to him flung themselves belly down and aimed a fusillade of bullets at the head and shoulders visible above the hole in the ground. The head exploded into a spray of blood and flying bone, and the weapon was dropped. Then the shoulders of the VC, supporting only the bloody stump of the neck, sank down into the hole and the trapdoor slammed back down over it.

Instantly, Dead-eye was up and running, weaving erratically from left to right to avoid any other snipers, and soon he was at the hole. He raised the trapdoor and, without looking in, dropped in a hand-grenade, then threw himself backwards, well away from the imminent explosion.

As soil and smoke spewed upwards from the hole and rained back down over Dead-eye, the rest of the men raced forward, spread well apart, to check if any other guerrillas were in the vicinity.

There were.

All over this sea of black shell holes and scorched corpses, trapdoors was opening to allow snipers to pop up and unleash fire on the SAS men. Even worse, the savage roar of a 7.62mm RPD light machine-gun was suddenly added to the bedlam.

No sooner had Blue knelt beside his butchered sergeant, checking if he was still alive – he wasn't – than he was punched back by a hail of bullets from the machine-gun and slammed on to his back. Bleeding profusely from the belly, but still alive, he was groping for his automatic rifle as Dead-eye and Shagger, running side by side and clearly thinking alike, simultaneously threw a couple of hand-grenades towards where they could see the VC machine-gun winking, behind a natural barricade of upturned earth.

The grenades exploded at the same time with a mighty crash, sending loose soil spewing through clouds of smoke. Even before the smoke and dust had cleared, Shagger and Dead-eye were running towards the gun emplacement, Red was calling on the radio for the medics and reinforcements from 1 and 3 SAS Squadrons, the wounded Blue was crawling into the relative safety of a shell hole, leaving a trail of blood behind him, and the others were giving covering fire to Shagger and Dead-eye.

These two had reached the rim of the enemy gun position and were firing their automatic rifles into it without bothering to check that anyone was still alive. In fact, the gunner had been on his own and was now lying on his side beside his overturned machine-gun. Half of his jaw had been blown away and one hand had been mangled into a bloody mess. The flies were already swarming over him when Shagger and Dead-eye clambered up the other side of the trench, looked across a lunar landscape of shell holes, and saw more VC firing at them from holes in the ground, their heads and shoulders framed by raised trapdoors.

'We can't eliminate them on our own,' Dead-eye said.

'1 and 3 Squadrons are on their way,' Shagger answered.

'Even they'll get decimated,' Dead-eye said. 'We need the tanks to go ahead of us and take that lot out.'

'I agree,' Shagger said. Turning back, he used a hand signal to indicate that Red should come up with the PRC 64. Red strapped the radio on to his back, picked up his automatic rifle, carefully studied the enemy positions, then jumped out of his shell hole and ran at the crouch, zigzagging from one shell hole to the next.

Instantly, the VC snipers opened fire, trying to hit him. They, in turn, received a barrage of fire from the combined weapons of the SAS men. Nevertheless, many of the guerrillas kept firing and bullets were still kicking up the soil around Red as he threw himself down beside Shagger and Dead-eye.

'Good enough for the Olympics,' Shagger said, grinning, to the breathless Red. 'You looked like you had a bee up the arse and were trying to fart it out.'

'Rather a bee up my arse than a bullet,' Red replied without rancour, unstrapping the radio.

At that moment another wave of semi-automatic fire came from the many VC hides, obviously aimed at somewhere behind the SAS men. Glancing back over their shoulders, they saw Jimbo zigzagging towards them, disappearing down into shell holes, then racing up and out again, desperately dodging the lines of soil and stones that whipped up on both sides of him. Miraculously, he managed to reach their position and threw himself down beside them, automatically tugging the peak of the slanting jungle hat from his eyes and gratefully gulping air into his lungs.

'Jesus Christ!' he gasped. 'Where did all those bastards come from? They must have stayed in those covered holes all night, through the air attacks and bombardments. Fucking unbelievable!'

'Right,' Red said. 'If they weren't completely deafened by the noise, they should have been driven crazy.'

'They don't seem very crazy to me,' Jimbo told him. 'Not the way they're firing those rifles. All those bastards are fighting fit.'

'Contact Callaghan,' Shagger told Red. 'Then give me the phone.' When Red had contacted the lieutenant-colonel and handed Shagger the phone, Shagger said, 'Sergeant Bannerman here, boss.'

'Yes, Sergeant. What's happening?'

'We're faced with a field filled with VC snipers in trapdoor hides. They've got us pinned down. To clear them out, we need those Centurions and reinforcements in APCs. We can't cross that field unprotected; it would just be a slaughter.'

'Tanks and APCs coming up immediately,' Callaghan confirmed. 'But I still need you men out front to recce the airfield. If you can't cross that field, can you go around it?'

Shagger studied the terrain ahead, then checked his map. 'Possibly,' he told Callaghan. 'We'll try and circle around it and close in on the airfield. If the tanks and APCs leave right now, they should arrive here just as we get to the other side.'

'Then advance on the airfield,' Callaghan said. 'Over and out.'

Handing the phone back to Red, Shagger picked up his M16A1 and said, 'OK, let's do it. Red, you stick with Dead-eye and me; I may need the radio again. We'll circle around to the south-west of the field. Jimbo, you join the remaining two men from Team 2 and circle around in the opposite direction. When we converge at the far side, we'll move in on the airfield together.'

'Right,' Jimbo said.

Suddenly the enemy snipers opened fire *en masse* and sent a hail of bullets whining over the heads of the four SAS men. Glancing back over their shoulders, they saw that an advance team from either 1 or 3 SAS Squadron, perhaps a mixture of both, was making its way between the shell holes, some of the men firing their personal weapons to give cover to the medical team carrying rolled-up stretchers. A smoke flare shot up from the shell hole where the badly wounded Blue had taken refuge, indicating that he was still alive and showing exactly where he was. Immediately, the medical team changed direction, zigzagging from one hole to another and gradually advancing on the one where the corporal lay. As they did so, the SAS men around them gave covering fire by jumping to their feet, firing a quick burst, then dropping behind what shelter they could find, all the time advancing slowly. To give them further support, Shagger and the others also opened fire on the enemy positions, pinning them down long enough for the SAS medical team to reach Blue's shell hole and roll down into it, beside him. The other SAS men followed suit, then crawled up to the lip of the hole to fire at the VC. At this point Shagger and his men stopped firing.

'Are you ready to go, Jimbo?' Dead-eye asked.

Jimbo glanced to his right and saw Norton and Mad Mike waving at him from a hole about thirty yards away. Turning back to Dead-eye, he nodded and jerked his thumb in the air.

'Right,' Dead-eye said. 'We'll give you covering fire. Get going the minute we open up.' He glanced at Shagger and received a curt nod.

'*Now!*' Shagger barked.

The three SAS men opened fire simultaneously, sending a hail of bullets into the VC positions, moving their weapons from left to right, up and down, to sweep across the whole target. Instantly, Jimbo jumped up and ran hell for leather towards Norton and Mad Mike, who had also opened fire to lend their support. Though many of the VC were forced to remain in their holes as bullets churned up the earth about them, the more foolhardy or courageous still threw their camouflaged trapdoors up and popped up to try to pick Jimbo off.

They almost succeeded. Bullets were stitching the ground ever nearer to Jimbo when he was only halfway through his run. Just before the spitting lines converged on the imagined track he was racing along, he threw himself down into the nearest shell hole. The guerrillas' bullets converged where he had been, turning the spot into a chaos of exploding soil and swirling dust as he rolled down to the bottom of the hole, scrambled up the other side and prepared to make the second half of the run.

The combined weapons of the SAS, including those of the men protecting the medical team, created a deafening bedlam as they poured a hail of bullets into the guerrillas. Many dropped out of sight, but others had their heads blown apart and the trapdoors shot to splinters before they, too, dropped down out of sight. Under that deadly covering fire, Jimbo jumped up and ran, crouching low and zigzagging again, this time making it all the way to Norton and Mad Mike without stopping. Soon he was lying belly down beside them.

'Nice one,' Mad Mike said with what seemed like a crazy leer. 'You ran like the wind, mate.'

'With good reason,' Jimbo replied.

'So what's the state of play?' Norton asked.

Jimbo jabbed his finger in the direction they were to take. 'We're going to circle around this lot and join up with Team 1 at the far side of the field, between the field and the airfield.'

'What about this bunch?' Norton asked, indicating the VC still popping up occasionally to take pot-shots at the SAS men. 'We just leave them to slaughter the men coming up after us?'

'No. That's been taken care of. The men directly behind us are staying put until the field is cleared by a couple of Centurions and some APCs. They'll only advance when that's done. By which time we should have reached the airfield and can guide them in there.'

'Fair enough,' Norton said. 'We go now?'

'Yeah,' Jimbo said. 'When I signal the others to give us covering fire, we get up and run. Once we get to the shelter of those trees at the side of the field, we should be OK.'

Norton scanned the line of badly burnt trees that ran alongside the devastated paddy-field. He nodded consent.

Jimbo used a hand signal to indicate that the other SAS men should open fire. The minute they did so, creating a dreadful racket, Jimbo and the two men from Team 2 jumped out and ran at the crouch, zigzagging towards the trees at the side of the field. VC bullets kicked up the earth all around them, but none of them was hit and soon they were crashing through what was left of the scorched undergrowth of the tree line, where they temporarily rested.

Seeing that they were safe, the rest of the SAS men stopped firing and Shagger's team prepared to make a similar run in the opposite direction. Hearing the silence of the SAS guns, an occasional VC sniper would pop up and let off another shot, either at the SAS men in front or at the trees, sending the occasional bullet ricocheting off a tree trunk or scorched, leafless branch. However, Jimbo and the other two were well protected by the trees and, once they had got their breath back, were able to march on unmolested, circling around to the back of the field and the route that led to the airfield.

As Jimbo's team melted into the trees at the far side of the field, Shagger gave a hand signal and the SAS men protecting the medical team around Blue opened fire on the VC poking out of their hides, pinning enough of them down to enable Shagger and the others to jump up and race across the field as the bullets of the bolder guerrillas tore up the ground at their feet.

This time, however, a VC popped out of his hole, dragging the long stem of an RPG7V grenade launcher on to his shoulder. He managed to aim at the running men and fire just before a ferocious burst of SAS fire hammered into him, making him shudder dramatically, drop the grenade launcher and sink back into the hole as the raised trapdoor behind him disintegrated under the same hail of bullets. Simultaneously, the rocket-propelled grenade, leaving a stream of smoke behind it, exploded with a deafening roar just short of the running men. Almost bowled off their feet by the blast, they were then choked and temporarily blinded by the cloud of dust and gravel that swept over them. Burdened by his radio, Red staggered sideways and stopped, but immediately hurled himself forward again when a stream of bullets stitched a line towards him, almost clipping his boot heels.

Bursting out of the cloud of dust and fine gravel, the three men continued zigzagging until they reached the cover of the trees. Once there, they turned and circled the field in a north-easterly direction, well away from the VC hides, from where small arms could still be heard firing in a more sporadic manner. Eventually, after an uneventful ten minutes, they were able to turn right, now protected by another line of trees and the stunted remains of what had been a dense patch of jungle. Shagger called them to a halt with a hand signal, then drew them together for a whispered talk.

'It's not over yet,' he said. 'There could be more snipers or booby-traps in this stretch.'

'I doubt it,' Dead-eye replied, indicating the smashed, stunted, charred trees all around them. 'This bit of jungle has been practically flattened by the bombs and twenty-five-pounders. Our main problem is climbing over the fallen branches and foliage. There's an awful lot of it.'

That was true enough. The ground between the destroyed trees was covered with mounds of smashed tree trunks, torn-off branches and burnt foliage, much of it little more than ash. When Red tentatively tapped some of this ash with the point of his boot, it rose up in a cloud.

'Bloody hell,' he said. 'We could choke to death getting through this shit.'

'We've got to do it,' Shagger said quietly. 'So come on, let's get going.'

They started their hike along the edge of the field, and immediately, as they clambered over the first pile of debris, the fine ash kicked up by their boots billowed all around them. As they continued to advance, it drifted around their faces, getting into their noses and lungs, making them choke and cough. But they had to keep going, scaling the mounds of debris, slipping and sliding down the other side, crossing a welcome stretch of relatively clear ground, then starting the whole process over again, all the while coughing and sneezing from the drifting ash.

They were halfway to the RV with Jimbo's team when they heard the pounding of heavy guns, followed instantly by the harsh chatter of machine-guns of various calibres. Glancing across the field, they saw two fifty-ton Centurion Mark Vs of the Australian 5th and 6th Battalions trundling towards the VC hides, each firing its single twenty-pounder gun, a .50-calibre Browning ranging machine-gun, and two .30-calibre Browning machine-guns while on the move.

When the first shells fell among the VC positions, the whole field appeared to erupt into flames and boiling smoke. Even so, some of the trapdoors remained open and the occupants of those hides continued recklessly to fire their weapons, though most of them were almost instantly shot to shreds by the Centurions' machine-guns.

By the time the tanks had reached the first of the hides, half a dozen M113A1 armoured personnel carriers, which looked similar to the tanks but lacked the high, revolving turret, came into view, following them into the field. The APCs had a crew of two, were capable of carrying up to eleven troops, and were also equipped with a .30-calibre and .50-calibre machine-gun combination mounted on the turret, as well as a 76mm machine-gun.

As the tanks rumbled over the hides, making the first of them cave in and crushing the occupants to death, other trapdoors flipped open and the black-clad snipers hurriedly scrambled out and tried to escape. This they did too late, however, for by the time they were out and running, the APCs had overtaken the Centurions and were spreading out to mow them down with their machine-guns. Those same weapons were also pumping a hail of bullets into every visible hide, whether opened or not, and turning the ground into a hell of swirling soil and dust.

Some of the VC desperately tried to roll hand-grenades under the steel treads of the tanks, but in most cases were shot down before they could do so, while some of them were blown up by their own grenades. Others tried to clamber up the rear of the tanks, but if they were not riddled by the machine-guns of the passing APCs, they lost their grip and fell off, to die screaming as they were crushed horribly under the treads.

Finally, when most of the visible VC were either dead or badly wounded, the men of 1 and 3 SAS Squadrons swarmed out of the APCs and began to check both the guerrillas on the ground and those in the remaining holes, to ensure that no survivors were still hidden down there. If they had the slightest reason to suspect that there were, they either fired their semi-automatic weapons down into the holes or dropped hand-grenades in and hared away.

This grim mopping-up procedure was still in progress as Shagger, Dead-eye and Red met Jimbo, Norton and Mad Mike at the RV.

'Christ,' Jimbo said, glancing back at that grim field of death. 'What an unholy slaughter!'

'Rather them than us,' Shagger said. 'Now let's get to that airfield.'

12

Even viewed from a distance of 500 yards through Shagger's binoculars, the VC airfield was clearly a makeshift affair hastily thrown up after they had captured the nearby village. The nominal perimeter was delineated by sandbagged gun emplacements manned by two-man teams armed with Chincom 57mm recoilless rifles, 7.62mm RPD light machine-guns and RPG7V rocket-propelled grenade launchers. But there was no fence of any kind – only barbed-wire entanglements spread along the ground – and the aircraft sat on a levelled field at the edge of the camp, which consisted of a thatched-roofed control tower raised on stilts, a similarly constructed water tower, and a wide variety of tents.

Fuel tankers were standing close by the aircraft, nearly a dozen troop trucks were parked near the tents, and dozens of VC soldiers, most wearing black fatigues, many armed with AK47s, were either resting by their tents, working at various tasks, or on guard outside the perimeter, between the gun emplacements. Beyond the airstrip, framed by the green of untouched jungle, lay the village, a cluster of concrete-and-tile houses inhabited by the Vietnamese who worked in the surrounding rubber plantations.

The SAS men were hiding behind a slight dip in the irrigated field that ran out to the edge of the airfield. Furrowed and muddy from recent heavy rain, the field contained many protective hollows, though most were filled with water.

'Judging by the number of trucks,' Shagger said, 'I'd say there were too many of them for us to take out alone.'

'I agree,' Dead-eye said. 'But we can still do a fair amount of damage – or at least harassment – with the help of 1 and 3 SAS, including those tanks and APCs, while the 5th and 6th Battalions are getting here. That way, we stand a chance of taking that village before last light.'

Shagger checked his watch. It was almost noon. 'I agree. Let's call up the SAS immediately and request that 5th and 6th Battalions be lifted in as soon as possible. Get HQ for me, Red.' When Red had given him the telephone, Shagger spoke to Callaghan, who agreed to order SAS reinforcements immediately and confirmed that he would contact HQ at Nui Dat and get 5th and 6th Battalions lifted out as soon as the helicopters could be prepared.

'Are you going to pave the way?' Callaghan asked.

'Yes, boss,' Shagger said.

'Good,' Callaghan said. 'Best of luck. Over and out.'

Handing the telephone back to Red, Shagger glanced across at the airfield and said, 'As 1 and 3 Squadrons are travelling in the APCs, they should make it here even quicker than we did. That means they should be here in about fifteen minutes. There's not much we can do until they get here except have a quick lunch – though it has to be cold. We don't want smoke from a brew-up. Not even cigarettes.'

The last comment drew exaggerated groans from the men gathered around Shagger.

'Shut up, you whinging drongos,' he said, 'and have something to eat while you can. Wash it down with cold water and be grateful to get it.'

'The way I feel, I'd be grateful to drink my own piss,' Jimbo said.

'Worked up a thirst, have you?' said Mad Mike.

'Throat's as dry as a camel's arse,' Jimbo informed him.

'Grew familiar in North Africa, did you?' Red asked. 'Got desperate out in the desert and explored forbidden territory, eh?'

'Up yours!' Jimbo exclaimed.

'We were talking about the camel's,' Mad Mike said.

'I never even rode a fucking camel. Couldn't stand the smell of them. Not my type at all, mate. Of course, the smell wouldn't have put you off. Your own smell would have smothered it.'

'I take a bath at least once a month, whether I need it or not,' Mad Mike said.

'Yeah,' Jimbo retorted. 'I've heard that the Aussie SAS demand a high standard of hygiene when they give each other their nightly blow-jobs.'

The Aussies burst out laughing, then Mad Mike placed his hand on Jimbo's shoulder and shook him affectionately. 'Good on you, mate.'

Each man had selected his own quick, dry lunch from his survival belt, which included enough food and equipment for two days. Their lunch consisted of high-calorie rations, including chocolate, dried biscuits and cheese, washed down with water from their bottles.

No sooner had they returned the remaining rations to their survival belts than the Centurions and APCs came into view over the crest of a slope and lumbered towards them. Instantly, the men around Shagger and Dead-eye checked their personal weapons, spread out along the incline, and prepared to follow the approaching vehicles into the airfield.

161

In fact, even before it had reached the men hidden by the slight incline, the convoy was inevitably spotted by the VC and the dull pounding of three or four grenade launchers was heard as they were fired in quick succession. Within seconds, the smoke trails of four rocket-propelled grenades made languid arcs in the air and then looped down towards the tanks and APCs. Explosions tore up the ground between the vehicles, showering them with raining soil, but still they advanced. As more grenades started falling, the armoured vehicles were forced to weave wildly to make themselves more difficult targets, but eventually they reached the SAS team lying on the incline.

The captain of the leading tank, a 5th Battalion lieutenant, opened the turret to reveal himself from the shoulders up, and said to Shagger, 'We're going straight in, with the APCs behind us. I suggest you take cover behind them. When we reach the enemy forces in the airfield, your mates will dismount from the APCs and tackle the enemy forces on the ground while we blow the aircraft and transport to hell. Best of luck, lads.'

Just as the lieutenant dropped back down through the hatch, pulling the lid shut behind him, a series of grenades exploded short of the tanks and APCs, nearly deafening the men on the ground, pummelling them with the combined blasts, and raining soil and stones down on them. Hugging the earth, they watched as the steel treads of the armoured vehicles started turning, cutting deep grooves in the soil, until the vehicles were lurching away from the incline, towards the airfield – first the tanks, then the APCs. Once they were past, Shagger and the other men jumped to their feet and ran at the half crouch to take cover behind the latter.

As they were normally on their own, and usually well out in front of the main forces, this was an unusual position for the SAS to be in. But they stuck close to the rear of the advancing APCs as the enemy's grenades continued to explode all around them. These were followed immediately by the harsh chatter of their light machine-guns and recoilless rifles, which caused bullets to ricochet noisily off the vehicles.

Within seconds, however, when the tanks and APCs had spread well apart to form a long, well-spaced line, the tanks were returning the enemy fire with their twenty-pound guns and the combined ferocity of their .30-calibre, .50-calibre and 76mm machine-guns. In less than a second the enemy gun positions were obscured by showering soil and thick black smoke.

As was bound to happen, a VC grenade struck one of the tanks, exploding low on the front, blowing off both treads and shrouding it in smoke. The men inside were not hurt and as the tank shuddered to a standstill, with flames licking from its underside, they scrambled one after the other out of the turret, slid down the side and raced away. The other vehicles were already giving the flaming, smoking tank a wide berth when it exploded as a great ball of fire covered by an umbrella of black, oily smoke.

As if in instant reprisal, one of the shells from a Centurion's twenty-pounder blew a VC gun emplacement apart, hurling men into the air, along with exploding sandbags, soil and pebbles.

As the tanks neared the gun positions, with the APCs close behind them, Dead-eye started jumping out from behind the protection of his APC to fire short bursts at the black-shirted figures he saw running to and fro, carrying AK47s. Relieved to see many of them throw their arms up, drop their weapons, shudder or spin sideways and fall down, the other SAS men followed Dead-eye's example and started firing too.

One of the APCs was hit by a grenade, the explosion erupting beneath its front, lifting it briefly off the ground, then slewing it sideways in a cloud of oily smoke. As fierce yellow flames shot out from a punctured petrol can, the men inside, all from 3 SAS Squadron, clambered one after the other out of the turret and slid to the ground.

But before the last two could get out, a hail of VC bullets rattled off the APC with a horrible drumming sound and the first man was thrown back violently. He writhed spasmodically for a few seconds, screaming in agony as bullets punched into his body, then rolled down the front of the vehicle and fell to the ground with a thud.

The trooper behind him was just emerging when a second barrage of bullets ricocheted off the vehicle, some turning his head into a mess of blood and bone, and he fell back into the APC without a sound.

The men who had escaped the damaged APC were spreading out, holding their weapons at the ready, when it exploded with a muffled thump, shook violently and became a ball of bright-yellow flames and dense black smoke. The men were briefly obscured by the smoke, but when it cleared they could be seen still spreading out and now advancing on the enemy positions by running in short bursts, firing their semi-automatic weapons from the hip, then throwing themselves to the ground each time the enemy returned fire. Some were hit, but the others kept advancing.

The first of the Centurions passed over the perimeter created by the line of VC gun emplacements and were soon followed by the APCs. As the tanks continued rumbling towards the airstrip, the APCs stopped between the emplacements and poured a hail of machine-gun fire into them, enabling the men inside to clamber out through the turret and drop to the ground, where they engaged the enemy in close quarter battle.

'Let's go!' Shagger bawled.

He and the others raced towards the VC still remaining in the sunken gun positions, blasting away at them while on the move. The savage roar of the VC machine-gun was silenced when Jimbo threw a hand-grenade that landed right in the middle of the emplacement and blew the weapon to pieces, filling the air with the swirling sand from exploded sandbags and leaving the two gunners dead. Some of the VC continued firing from their gun positions until they were dispatched with automatic rifle fire at short range; others, in desperation, sprang out swinging machetes. As the SAS men had no bayonets on their weapons, they simply jumped back out of range and shot down their assailants at close range.

Dead-eye was running towards a VC gun position, firing from the hip, when he was deafened by a fearsome roar, hammered by an invisible force, then felt himself being picked up and hurled back down again. Hitting the ground hard, he blacked out for a few seconds. On regaining consciousness, he found himself lying on his back, covered with soil and still trying to recover his breath.

Just as he was gathering his senses, a guerrilla materialized directly above him, a youth of no more than sixteen, holding a machete on high, about to bring it down on his head. Rolling away just as the weapon thudded into the ground where his head had been, Dead-eye swiftly removed his 9mm Browning High Power handgun from its holster, came to rest on his back, steadied himself by bending his knees and pressing his feet on the ground, then fired up at the guerrilla before he could swing the machete again.

Though the first bullet hit the attacker in the chest and punched him back, Dead-eye kept firing until he had fallen and was making no movement; then he jumped back to his feet, picked up his SLR, and advanced on the nearest gun emplacement. He was now firing his SLR with his right hand, the stock tucked into his waist, while also firing single shots from the Browning in his left.

The VC in the emplacement annihilated, Dead-eye moved on. By now the Centurions were blasting the parked aircraft with their twenty-five-pounders and explosions were ripping up the runway. First one, then another aircraft burst into sheets of flame and rolling clouds of smoke, with debris flying through the air in all directions to become yet another hazard to the VC on the ground.

As the aircraft were exploding, more guerrillas were racing out of the tents, many firing their weapons on the run. Two machine-guns located near the tents also opened fire, forcing the SAS men to throw themselves to the ground.

'We need air support,' Dead-eye told Shagger.

'Bloody oath, we do. *Red!* Get on to Callaghan and then give me the phone.' Red did as he was told, and Shagger told the CO exactly what he wanted.

'Pinned down, are you?' Callaghan asked.

'That's a mild way of putting it.'

Callaghan chuckled. 'Very good, Sergeant. The air support will be there in fifteen minutes, followed by 5th and 6th Battalions. Meanwhile, sit tight.'

'My very intention,' Shagger said.

He and the others sat tight by lying on their bellies and pouring a hail of bullets at the VC spreading over the flat ground between their tents and the SAS positions, most of them casting long shadows in the lights of the burning aircraft to the side. The tanks and APCs were now parked north of the SAS men and were concentrating on pounding the VC aircraft still untouched and the troop trucks nearby. Every so often one or the other would explode dramatically, while many were already ablaze and smoking. This, however, did not stop the relentless advance of around a hundred VC, all of whom were firing on the move and appeared not to care about their own losses.

However, well before the VC reached CQB positions, six USAF Phantom Jet F-4Cs appeared in the sky, coming from the directions of Nui Dat. One minute they were mere specks on the horizon, the next they were roaring in at low level to fire their rockets at the advancing VC and the enemy's remaining aircraft and vehicles. Within seconds, the oil tankers had been blown up and the airstrip had turned into a hell of searing yellow balls of fire, boiling black smoke, and running, screaming guerrillas, many of them on fire.

When the Phantoms circled around and returned to repeat the process, they targeted the raised control tower and water tower. The first rockets blasted through the control tower, blowing out its walls and setting fire to the collapsing roof, while the second pilot destroyed its base with deadly accuracy. His rockets blew the struts to pieces and caused the rest of the tower to first buckle, then break apart, with screaming men and navigation equipment raining down amid other flaming debris.

The third and fourth Phantoms concentrated on the tall water tower, blowing the tank to pieces, so that the water sprayed out in a silvery cascade that drenched the burning remains of the collapsed control tower and turned the flames into boiling clouds of steam. The fifth and sixth Phantoms then blew the struts of the water tower to pieces and left it collapsing as they banked for another run.

When the Phantoms circled around and returned for a third attack, creating even more hideous devastation, the VC who had been advancing on the SAS fled back towards the village, now barely visible through the smoke.

Shagger had just ordered his men to advance across the smoke-covered airstrip when a flock of black birds appeared on the horizon. These soon became recognizable as USAF Chinooks, bringing in the men of the 5th and 6th Battalions. Pleased to see the approaching choppers, Shagger and Dead-eye advanced side by side, protected by the tanks and APCs, across an airstrip pock-marked with ugly, black shell holes, many of which were filled with VC dead. They were followed by Jimbo and Red, then by Norton and Mad Mike, each two-man team staying close behind a tank or an APC, and repeatedly leaning out from the rear to fire short bursts from their automatic rifles. By now their targets were mere shadows in the murk, all running the other way.

When the Phantoms banked for the final time and flew away, leaving an inferno of flame and smoke on the runway, the tanks and APCs accelerated, the former to weave through the blazing aircraft, firing their machine-guns, the latter to pursue the fleeing VC beyond their blazing tents and on to the village.

Left behind by the armoured vehicles, but no longer threatened by the VC, Shagger and the others stopped for a break, drinking water and lighting up cigarettes, squinting through the smoke as the Chinooks descended over the scarred ground, each pilot looking for a landing space between the shell holes.

As the Chinooks touched down one by one, their spinning rotors made the smoke swirl eerie patterns that changed shape constantly. Buffeted by the violent slipstreams, the men on the ground covered their eyes with their hands or used handkerchiefs to keep the flying dust out of their mouths and nostrils. Soon the men of 5th and 6th Battalions were marching down the rear ramps of the Chinooks, leaning into the beating wind being created by the still spinning rotors and likewise shielding their eyes from the swirling clouds of dust. Shadowy as ghosts, they spread out around the choppers, forming into long, loose lines, to begin mopping up any remaining VC, before marching on to the village.

'While they're doing that,' Shagger said to Dead-eye, Jimbo and the others, 'we'll go on ahead and see if we can give them any advance info. Let's get up and go, men.'

'No fucking rest for the wicked,' Mad Mike said, wearily shaking his head from side to side as he clambered to his feet and ground his cigarette with his boot.

'You're the man to know that,' Norton informed him. 'You're paying for your sins.'

'We're *all* paying for our sins,' Shagger said. 'Every day of our fucking lives. OK, men, move out.'

As the men headed off through the smoke, following the tanks and APCs towards the village, two RAAF Iroquois arrived with D6 bulldozers slung from cables beneath them. At the same time American loadmasters were offloading crates of equipment from the Chinooks.

Some of the 5th and 6th Battalion troops spread out to take over the captured airstrip. The rest, along with 1 and 2 SAS Squadrons, prepared to follow Shagger's advance party on to the VC stronghold, which was just about visible in the gathering night, beyond the pall of smoke.

13

Great clouds of dust hung over the airfield like a shroud, blown there by all the choppers ferrying men and equipment in, as the SAS men left it behind. They had marched only about half the distance to the village when, to their surprise, the tanks and APCs up ahead stopped, some of the drivers popping up from the turrets and using hand signals to indicate that they had been ordered to halt.

'What the fuck are those drongos doing?' growled Shagger, studying the armoured vehicles and then squinting at the blood-red sun dipping towards the horizon. 'We've got to take that damn village by nightfall.'

'Incoming message,' Red informed him. 'Lieutenant-Colonel Callaghan. He must have left the bunker complex and come up here. There's an awful lot of static in the background, so I think he's calling from a moving vehicle – probably 5th or 6th Battalion. Anyway he's not far away.'

With Dead-eye and Jimbo looking thoughtfully at him, Shagger took the microphone from Red and said, 'Yes, boss. Sergeant Bannerman here.'

'I've ordered all the vehicles to stop their advance on the village. I want you to stop as well. Stick close to them, but don't move on the village until I get there. I'll be with you in ten minutes for a briefing.'

'Right, boss,' Shagger said. 'Over and out.' He handed the microphone back to Red, shook his head from side to side, spat on the ground, then stared sardonically first at Jimbo, then at the impassive Dead-eye. 'We're stopping,' he said.

'What for?' Dead-eye asked.

'Another bloody briefing from our Pommy CO,' Shagger said. 'What the fuck do we need a briefing for now? We're practically on top of the village.'

'If Callaghan calls a briefing, it's usually important,' Dead-eye said.

'Maybe,' Shagger replied, not convinced. 'Anyway, we're to join the vehicles and wait for him there, so let's move our arses.'

They reached the convoy just as the drivers and SAS troops were hoisting themselves up through the turrets and clambering down to the ground. A few minutes later Callaghan arrived in a jeep that had clearly been flown in by one of the choppers and contained, in the back seats, two Vietnamese in black uniforms. When the jeep screeched to a halt, leaving deep grooves in the soft soil on the paddy-field, Callaghan, aware that he was presently out of range of the VC guns in the village, stood on his seat and called the men around him.

'I know you're all anxious to take the village,' he said, 'but I thought you should know a few facts first.' This opening statement was greeted with a mixture of applause and sardonic comments. When the noise had died down Callaghan continued. 'Intelligence has estimated that the village was being controlled by a VC company of about a hundred men. That figure has now increased by approximately fifty per cent by the VC who've just fled the airfield.'

'No sweat, boss,' Jimbo said. 'We can still take them on.'

'I trust so. But you should know that this target was part of a US Strategic Hamlet Program, which removed people from their traditional villages and resettled them in fortified hamlets. For that very reason, it's surrounded by mines, booby-traps, a moat and a palisade of wooden stakes. The Yanks put them there for the protection of the village and now, ironically, they're going to be our biggest obstacle in recapturing it.'

'We can still do it, boss,' Shagger said with conviction.

Callaghan grinned and nodded. 'I like your attitude, Sarge, but it's not going to be as easy as you think.'

'What's the plan then, boss?'

'Well, it involves staging a noisy frontal feint along the road towards the main gate – that's the job of the SAS – while the 5th and 6th Battalions carry out the actual assault from the rear. The manoeuvre to get in position for the rear assault can only be carried out with great stealth, slowly and on foot, by following a wide arc around the village. It should take the 5th and 6th a few hours to complete this. Meanwhile the SAS, led by myself, will penetrate the palisade and secure a foothold while another platoon makes the first assault.'

'There's not a fence we can't get through,' Dead-eye said flatly.

'That may be true enough,' Callaghan replied, 'but we first have to find a safe way through the booby-trapped barrier that skirts the village. For this, I'm planning to use these two gentlemen' – he waved his hand at the two prisoners sitting solemnly in the back of the jeep – 'both of whom are VC defectors from the village. Guided by them, I think we can make it in.'

'When?' Dead-eye asked.

'Why wait?' Callaghan replied, to Dead-eye's obvious relief. 'We have the complete contingent of 1 and 3 SAS right here, backed up by the 5th and 6th. We move in right now, before last light, and clear the whole damn village. What say you, gentlemen?'

'I say yes,' said Dead-eye.

'I second that,' Jimbo said.

'Anything a Pom can do, we can do,' Shagger added.

'Then let's do it,' Callaghan said. He climbed down from the jeep and indicated that the VC defectors do the same. When they were on the ground beside him, he turned to Shagger and said, 'All right, Sergeant, we'll follow these gentlemen in. The rest of 1 and 3 Squadrons will be right there behind us. The 5th and 6th Battalions are already on their way here from the airstrip and I'll be keeping in touch with them by field phone. We'll make the frontal assault, breaching the palisade, while the 5th and 6th encircle the village and make the major assault from the rear.'

'Trust the regular army to choose the rear passage,' Jimbo whispered to Red. 'That says it all, don't it?'

'Just like the navy,' Red replied.

At that moment, a convoy of trucks came across the cleared path in the minefield, bringing the 5th and 6th Battalions from the captured airstrip. When the trucks had ground to a halt, the heavily armed soldiers of the two battalions poured out and formed into groups of a size that would form manageable single-file patrols through the rubber plantation, all the way round to the back of the village.

Callaghan walked over to have a word with the senior officers of the two battalions. Then, after what appeared to Shagger and Dead-eye to have been an extremely animated conversation, he returned to his own men.

'Right,' he said. 'The 5th and 6th are going to encircle the village and come up on its rear. However, we have to engage the enemy before they do, to cause a distraction. We've no time to waste, so let's move out immediately. The scouts will go first' – he paused and indicted the two Vietnamese – 'out on point, as it were, to guide us through the minefield and point out booby-traps, and the tanks and APCs will follow, with most of the men in the latter for protection.'

'*Most* of the men?' Shagger asked.

Callaghan looked steadily at him, then offered a tight smile. 'Yes, Sergeant,' he said. '*Most* of the men. The others – by which I mean you six – will go ahead with me and the VC scouts to ensure that they do what they should do and to relay back to the main forces anything we see while we're up at the front. Any problems, Sergeant?'

Shagger returned Callaghan's steady gaze for several seconds, then, accepting the challenge, even appreciating it, he said, 'No problem, boss. Where you lead, we will follow.'

'Good man.'

Turning to the VC guides, Callaghan nodded towards the village, and they loped away with the grace of deer. Callaghan then told Shagger and the other five men to fall in behind them. When they had done so, and were also heading towards the village, which was now sinking into an eerie, though less smoky twilight, Callaghan used a hand signal to order the tanks and APCs to follow the men on foot. The engines of the armoured vehicles rumbled into life and they advanced spread out in a long line, but moving slowly, keeping well behind the men on foot, to avoid mines and booby-traps.

In front, spread out in a well-spaced line just behind the sharp-eyed Vietnamese scouts, Shagger and the others had their automatic rifles at the ready and were likewise constantly alert for mines or booby-traps.

In Jimbo's mind this extra precaution was wholly justified. 'How the fuck can you trust them?' he asked. 'Those snaky little bastards could be leading us right on to the mines instead of guiding us through them.'

'Listen, mate,' Red replied. 'If you knew what would happen to those poor bastards if their VC friends caught them, you'd know just what kind of chance they've taken to come over to our side. They're not going to lead you on to any mines. No, they'll make sure we capture that village and wipe out the VC. That way they'll save their own arses. You can trust them, believe me.'

'*I* believe you,' Mad Mike said. 'But I still feel shit-scared of those mines. Can't help myself, fellas.'

'You're not worth a cuntful of cold water,' Red told him. 'All you'll lose if a mine goes off, mate, is your balls – and given your track record with the ladies, they're probably not worth worrying about.'

'Shut up, the lot of you,' Shagger whispered. 'This isn't a bloody exercise. It's the real thing. So zip your lips and keep your eyes to the front.'

'Right, Sarge,' both men whispered simultaneously.

They continued advancing behind the VC scouts and realized, with dread, that they were in the minefield when they saw them slowing down and casting their gazes to the ground.

'Christ!' Jimbo hissed.

'You've been through all this before, man,' Callaghan whispered.

'I'm OK, boss,' Jimbo replied. 'I'm just gulping some air in.'

'It helps,' Callaghan said.

They were crossing a broad, level paddy-field between the trees of rubber plantations and could see the village straight ahead, its brick-and-tile houses, surprisingly modern-looking, clearly outlined in the somnolent sunset, a slow and lazy dimming of air, deepening into darkness. Up ahead, the scouts were silhouetted in that changing light, repeatedly bending over to check the ground for mines and then straightening up to guide the armoured vehicles and SAS men forward with hand signals. The men walked gingerly, following the tracks of the armoured vehicles, but even the bravest of them could feel their hearts beating hard.

Twice they had to stop when the scouts pointed out booby-traps, planted right in the middle of the minefield: first a punji pit with a camouflaged tilting lid and then an angled arrow trap, concealed in a hole in the ground. They also stopped frequently to stick flagged markers into the ground on both sides of the tank and APC tracks, to show the way through the minefield to the 5th and 6th Battalion troops coming up behind them.

The hike across the minefield seemed to take for ever and was rendered even more nerve-racking by the failing light and the fact that they were now doing it in full view of the village, which was growing nearer all the time.

They came off the minefield just as darkness was falling. Knowing that his men couldn't attempt to cross the moat or breach the palisade in the darkness, Callaghan ordered the vehicles to halt, then called the men together for a Chinese parliament.

'It's taken longer than I envisaged and we can't see a damn thing in this darkness,' he said. 'So I believe we should settle in for the night and attack at first light. What do you think, men?'

'I agree, boss,' Dead-eye said. 'Not even these two VC turn-coats can see in the dark. We'd either get blown to hell by mines or nobbled by booby-traps. First light seems right to me.'

'I agree,' Shagger said, then glanced at the other men and received their nods of consent. Turning back to Callaghan, he said, 'We're all agreed, boss.'

'Good,' Callaghan said. 'Then let's bunk down right here. Shallow scrapes for sleeping and guards posted on all sides, two hours on, two hours off. No cigarettes, no fires, only cold rations. I'll get in touch with the 5th and 6th to let them know what we're doing.'

On making contact with the CO of the combined 5th and 6th, Callaghan informed him of what he and his men had decided. Lieutenant-Colonel Chambers, normally the CO of the 6th, now acting CO for both battalions, agreed that the idea was sound and said that he would position his men at the rear of the village, but keep them on hold until first light and, even then, not attack until he heard the sounds of engagement between Callaghan's men and the enemy.

Satisfied, Callaghan then ordered his demolitions men to lay a line of claymores along an invisible perimeter separating the makeshift camp from the route to the village. Activated by a trip-wire about 500 yards long, each mine would fire approximately 350 metal balls over a fan-shaped area up to a range of 100 yards, shredding anything in its path.

Callaghan went off to have tea with his fellow officers, all sitting on the ground near some rubber trees in the gathering darkness. His men, meanwhile, both English and Australian, were either digging their shallow scrape, covering it with a vacuum-compressed plastic sheet, or unrolling a sleeping-bag on to the sheet, depending upon how quick they were or how eager they were to bed down.

178

'I'm shagged,' Jimbo said, 'and I don't mind admitting it.'

'You always look shagged, mate,' said Red provocatively.

'You've only known me a few days.'

'It seems years to me, mate.'

'True love starts with the attraction of opposites, so there's hope for me yet.'

'Some Pommy nancy-boy, is he?' Mad Mike said to Red.

'I don't know, but I'm sleeping on my back tonight,' Red replied.

Chuckling, Jimbo pulled the sleeping-bag up to his chin and closed his eyes in the vain hope of sleep. In fact, he fell asleep quickly – as did the others around him – but none of them slept as long as they would have wished.

They were awakened just after midnight by the familiar, distant phut-phut of mortar fire, one mortar coming quickly after the other, like a growing drum roll. Even as they were opening their sleepy eyes, the first of the shells came hurtling down over their improvised camp and exploded all around them.

Pummelled by the blasts, stung by flying soil and stones, they hurriedly wriggled out of their sleeping-bags, picked up their rifles and rolled on to their bellies, trying to scan the night ahead.

The first waves of VC were charging directly at them in a surprise attack. Luckily, Callaghan's idea of laying clay-mores paid off when they ran straight on to them and the mines exploded, blowing some of the guerrillas apart and shredding the flesh of others with the hundreds of steel balls that flew upward at incredible speed.

Even as the mines were taking their terrible toll, the other VC were annihilated by withering sheets of automatic-rifle and machine-gun fire, backed by devastating blasts from the three different-calibre machine-guns on the APCs and

Centurions, as well as canister rounds from the latter. Similar to the claymores, the canister shots contained hundreds of ball-bearings which spread out in a murderous arc, scything down everything in their path. The devastation wrought by this combined onslaught on the advancing VC was appalling.

And yet they kept coming.

Hardly believing what he was seeing, Callaghan used the radio to call for artillery support from the Australian 105mm battery located back in the captured VC bunker complex, three miles away. In less than a minute shells were raining down on the VC, exploding in silvery-white flashes that briefly illuminated the darkness and then obscured the emerging moon and stars with their intermingling streams of dense smoke. Under that umbrella of smoke, scattering to avoid the explosions, the advancing VC melted into the trees on either side of the open stretch of ground that led to the village.

'One Squadron to the right!' Callaghan bawled. 'Three Squadron to the left!'

Before most of the other men could react, Dead-eye was running to the trees on the right, followed closely by Callaghan, Jimbo, then the startled Shagger, Norton, Red and Mad Mike, and finally by the rest of 1 Squadron. Once among the trees, where even the light of the stars was blotted out, they made their way forward, darting carefully from one tree to another, towards where they had seen the VC entering. To their surprise, since they had expected the VC to hide in the darkness, they had advanced only about four hundred yards when they saw a sea of flickering candles. These VC were carrying them as they made their way through the deepening darkness under the rubber trees.

Stunned by this surrealistic sight, most of the men looked on in disbelief. This collective trance was rudely broken by

Dead-eye, who without a second thought, opened fire with his SLR, delivering a short, exploratory burst. He was gratified to see a couple of the tiny flickering flames whip through the air before blinking out, indicating that he had hit the men holding them.

Almost as one, the rest of the SAS men followed suit and many of the candles were dropped to the ground as those holding them were either killed or threw them down to return the fire, their bullets thudding into the trees and showering the SAS men below them with foliage.

One SAS man was killed, then another.

Unable to see the enemy because their candles were dimmed, Callaghan instructed some of his men to send up flares. These burst like purple flowers above the trees to shed an eerie blue-and-crimson glow over the enemy, revealing that they were already withdrawing with their casualties, dragging them like sacks along the ground.

Realizing that he could not expect his men to advance through the dark jungle, prey to mines, booby-traps and VC snipers with infrared sights, Callaghan ordered a tactical withdrawal that would take them back to the two main battalions. This, however, was not as easy as it seemed because many of the VC had decided to stay in the jungle to harass the SAS with constant sniping.

One SAS man took a shot through the head and fell like a stone. Another was hit in the chest and punched backwards into a tree, then peppered with bullets even as he slid down the trunk, leaving a long smear of blood. A third kicked a trip-wire and was impaled on the half a dozen spikes of the booby-trap known as 'the whip'. Still standing upright, but quivering like a bowstring and pouring blood from his many wounds, he kept screaming dementedly until put out of his misery by a burst of VC machine-gun fire that practically tore him to shreds and actually punched him off the spikes and back down into the mud.

The slow, noisy, agonizing withdrawal took place in an eerie chiaroscuro: dark one instant, then brilliantly lit the next as flares were fired overhead to fall slowly, casting weird, distorted shadows on the trees. It took Callaghan's men two bloody hours, with substantial losses, to cover the 250 yards back through the perimeter.

At approximately four in the morning the battle tapered off as the surviving VC retreated to the village and Callaghan's team withdrew, knowing that they had to be well clear by first light and needed the time to look after their wounded and collect the dead.

Given that the medical team needed protection, Callaghan allotted his six best men – Shagger, Dead-eye, Norton, Jimbo, Red and Mad Mike – to accompany them. After making their way carefully back through the jungle, seeing only the odd glimmer of stars here and there through the canopy of trees, being acutely aware of the possible presence of mines and booby-traps, the men reached the area of the previous battle, where they formed a protective cordon around the medics as they went about their bloody business of picking up their wounded and dead.

Though no VC appeared in the jungle's enveloping darkness, the SAS men knew that they were nearby and engaged in exactly the same kind of grisly activity. This was confirmed when they heard what at first was a strange sound, but which became discernible as the creaking of wood. They realized at once that it was the sound of ox carts bearing away the VC casualties.

The medics, protected by the SAS men, remained in the jungle until just before dawn. As the sun's first pale rays fell on the jungle floor, they found the remains of about fifty guerrillas who had been missed in the darkness by their companions. Scattered among the dead were the meat-hooks which the VC had used to drag the bodies to the ox carts. Also found was a ghastly litter of human remains, clothing, equipment and shattered rubber trees, oozing latex and splattered with blood.

As it was not possible for the medics to remove all the bodies, they called for a team of Australian engineers to be flown in by chopper to bulldoze the bodies and other human remains into a mass grave. When this grisly task was completed, the SAS men returned to their makeshift camp to prepare for the attack on the village.

With the 5th and 6th Battalions now in position at the rear of the village, the battle to clear the area could begin.

14

The men moved against the village about an hour after dawn, hiking behind the Centurions and APCs as they rolled towards the moat they would have to cross. The VC, armed with AK47s, light machine-guns, and rocket-propelled grenade launchers, had taken aim through the wooden stakes of the palisade at the far side of the moat, but were holding fire until the SAS were within range.

Within minutes of the advance, the attacking vehicles had churned up clouds of red dust that both choked and obscured the men behind them, most of whom had wrapped scarves around their faces to keep out the dust. Even so, it blinded them, forcing them to stick close to the rear of the armoured vehicles. Therefore it came as a great relief to the men on foot when the vehicles suddenly roared louder and raced ahead and the tanks opened fire with their twenty-pounders and the APCs with their machine-guns.

The first of the shells from the tanks' big guns exploded, blowing whole sections out of the palisade, with broken stakes flying in all directions through the smoke and dead or wounded VC rolling down into the moat. Instantly, the other defenders opened fire with everything they had, including their Soviet-made grenade launchers.

As a hail of bullets was stitching the ground on both sides of the men marching behind the tanks and APCs, with other bullets clanging off the armoured bodies of the vehicles, a couple of grenades exploded between two of them, hurling up great columns of soil and dust, hammering the men behind the first vehicle with the blast. The tanks and APCs replied in kind, blowing more chunks out of the palisade and raking the rest of it with their machine-guns, tearing the stakes to shreds and filling the air with flying debris and dust.

By the time the vehicles had reached the edge of the moat, whole sections of the palisade had been blown open and the VC were edging away from it, shooting on the move as they were forced back into the village. There, as shells from the tanks' twenty-pounders exploded in the clearing between the houses, the inhabitants were cowering in their doorways or packing their belongings, before fleeing out the rear of the village.

At that moment, the tanks and APCs of 5th and 6th Battalion opened fire, raining a hail of shells on to the village which blew the walls out of some of the houses and caused more eruptions of soil and smoke in the clearing between them.

Shocked to find themselves being attacked from behind, some of the VC at the palisade turned away and hurried to the rear of the village, to take up defensive positions there. Even as they were doing so, the tanks and APCs of the 5th and 6th Battalions came into view, trundling towards the village with a mass of soldiers bunched up behind them, many already firing their assault rifles.

'Advance!' Callaghan bawled while using a hand signal to confirm the order for those out of earshot.

Unable to cross the water-filled moat, the vehicles kept up a continuous, murderous barrage of shells and machine-gun fire at the palisade, forcing the remaining VC back towards the village clearing while the SAS men slithered down the muddy bank and into the chest-high water.

Not all of them made it. The VC bold enough to stay at the palisade fired their last, defiant burst of gunfire and two or three of the SAS men were peppered with bullets, dropped their weapons and slithered into the water. As the medics slid down after them to check if they were dead or alive and, in the latter case, to prevent them from drowning, Callaghan and the other men waded across the moat, holding their weapons above their heads, then began the climb up the slippery slope on the other side.

Another shell exploded against what was left of the palisade, blowing it to pieces, and the attackers pressed themselves into the mud as the debris, including sharpened stakes, flew over their heads. Picking themselves up and wiping the mud from their faces, they resumed their climb and eventually made it to the top.

The Centurions and APCs stopped firing for fear of hitting their own men. Noting that the VC were retreating back into the centre of the village and that the tanks, APCs and men of 5th and 6th Battalions were advancing from the rear, Callaghan led his men in a charge against the village, firing their rifles and lobbing M26 high-explosive grenades.

The rest of 1 and 3 Squadron SAS came pounding after them.

Caught between the two advancing Australian forces, the VC began taking cover in the houses on either side of the clearing. As Callaghan, keen to fight his last battle to the utmost of his ability, rushed into one of the houses, firing his SLR from the hip, holding it in his left hand, and withdrawing his Browning handgun from his holster with the other, Shagger and Dead-eye, seeing VC snipers in the top windows of the same house, dropped to their knees and sent a hail of bullets into it. Plaster and powdered concrete exploded from around the window frame, someone screamed in agony, then the sniper's AK47 dropped to the street.

Jumping up again, Shagger and Dead-eye followed Callaghan into the house just as the latter kicked open the door of the downstairs living-room and fired a double-tap into the VC sniper he found lurking there. The man crashed backwards over a table, which collapsed beneath him, and fell on his back on the floor, where he lay still, his eyes open.

Callaghan was just backing out of the room when another VC sniper appeared at the top of the stairs. Even before Callaghan had seen him, Shagger and Dead-eye were firing simultaneously at him, the sound of their weapons shockingly loud in the small building, their bullets tearing the wooden stairs to shreds, splintering the unplastered brick walls, and turning the sniper into a shuddering, screaming mass of blood and exposed bone as he dropped his weapon and plunged headlong down the stairs to land at their feet.

'This house is cleared,' Callaghan said tersely. 'Let's move on to the next one.'

When they stepped back outside, they found the village centre filled with terrified, huddling peasants whom the VC were trying to use as human shields. This was not proving easy since the 5th and 6th Battalions were coming up on their rear even as 1 and 3 SAS Squadrons were advancing from the front, all of them firing on the move.

Leading off the square was a corrugated-iron church, from where some VC were firing down on the SAS troops with a light machine-gun. Jimbo and Red on one side of the short street, and Norton and Mad Mike on the other, were hiding in opposite doorways and taking pot-shots up at the church, but with little success.

Impatient, Callaghan grabbed a 66mm M72 rocket launcher from a passing trooper, balanced the cumbersome weapon expertly on his right shoulder, took aim and fired a rocket at the target, some 250 yards away. The weapon almost knocked him off his feet as it belched flame and smoke, but the rocket, bearing a high-explosive anti-tank warhead, sailed right over the church. Instead it erupted right in the middle of a bunch of VC who were running up the road on the other side of the church, hurling men and weapons in all directions and putting an abrupt stop to their advance.

The VC machine-gun in the church tower roared again, spraying a line of bullets down the incline, between the two teams crouched in opposite doorways, and missing Callaghan by inches.

Cursing softly, Callaghan braced himself and fired another rocket at the church. This time he scored a direct hit, blowing away most of the roof of the bell-tower, with the machine-gunner thrown out and hurled to the ground, his weapon falling beside him in a shower of debris. When the gunner had thudded into the unsurfaced street, Callaghan handed the weapon back to the trooper, patted him on the shoulder, then hand-signalled to the other men to follow him up the slope to the church.

As they reached the top of the hill, machine-guns roared and a blizzard of bullets turned the earth in front of them into a hell of spitting soil and swirling dust.

'Take cover!' Callaghan bawled.

Throwing themselves against the wall of the church just as the angry line of soil and dust raced past them, they saw that they had run into a platoon of VC stationed in fighting trenches on the high ground at the side of the church.

'We're fully exposed!' Shagger bawled.

'Let's go round to the front,' Dead-eye suggested.

They had just run away from the side wall and around to the front of the church when the side wall, fully exposed to the VC guns, received a barrage of bullets that sent lumps of plaster and pulverized cement flying in all directions. The wind picked the dust up and blew it into the front courtyard, where the men were taking up positions behind the side wall and peering carefully over it, between ornate steel railings, at the VC trenches.

'How many?' Callaghan asked.

'I'd say about thirty men in all,' Dead-eye replied. 'With two machine-gun emplacements.'

'Too many for us six,' Shagger observed.

'I agree,' Jimbo said.

'We step out there,' Red added, 'and those machine-guns will chop us to ribbons.'

'Yeah, chop suey,' Norton said. 'Not to my taste at all.'

'We need a gun bombardment,' Shagger said.

'Precisely aimed,' Dead-eye told him. 'Those trenches are only 500 yards away. We could cop it as well.'

'Bloody oath,' Shagger said.

All the men looked at Callaghan. He pursed his lips, tapped his knuckles against his teeth, screwed up his eyes and studied the VC fighting trenches, then sighed and said, 'Right.' After carefully checking his map, he told Red to contact the CO of the makeshift FOB being raised by the Aussies around the captured VC bunker complex. When Red had done so, Callaghan asked for a twenty-five-pounder barrage to be laid down on the nearby VC trenches, and gave very precise calibrations. 'Plug your ears, gentlemen,' he said as he handed the phone back to Red.

He wasn't joking. In less than five minutes the first shells from the big guns came whistling down over the church and slammed into the ground about 200 yards in front of the VC trenches. The shells exploded with a catastrophic bellowing, hurling soil and dust into the air and briefly obscuring the trenches in streams of smoke. When the smoke had cleared, the trenches appeared to be untouched.

'Too short,' Shagger observed.

'I *know* that, Callaghan said rather testily. He grabbed the phone from Red and got back in touch with the gunners at the bunker complex, to slightly modify the calibrations.

'You'll get it right on the button this time, boss,' Jimbo said encouragingly.

Callaghan said nothing.

Moments later the second round of shells exploded with the same deafening noise and again created immense showers of soil, dust and smoke. This time, however, the shells fell among the VC trenches, some of them direct hits, sending scorched bodies somersaulting through the smoke in a rainfall of debris – wooden planks, exploding sandbags, strips of burning clothing, scorched, dismembered limbs – to smash with dreadful impact into the ground.

Given confirmation that they now had the correct calibration, the gunners back in the bunker complex began a relentless, non-stop barrage that turned the trenches into a hell of erupting earth, scorching flames, choking smoke, and fragments of flying metal and wood. Remarkably, some of the VC had survived and were trying to make their exit from the few remaining untouched trenches.

'Open fire!' Shagger bawled.

Aiming through the iron railings of the side wall of the courtyard, the SAS opened fire with a murderous hail of bullets that cut down the guerrillas fleeing the trenches.

Suddenly, a shell from an Australian gun smashed through the remains of the bell-tower and exploded inside the church, blowing out part of the wall, deafening the SAS men, hitting them with flying bricks, cement and wood, and covering them with clouds of choking dust.

'Shit!' Red exclaimed.

Within seconds, more shells were exploding all around them, even one in the courtyard itself, and the men realized that one of the gun teams had for some reason changed its calibration and was now aiming at exactly where they were. With the church crumbling and explosions erupting about them, they had no choice but to move, so Callaghan, unable to make himself heard above the bedlam, used a hand signal to order an advance on the smoke-obscured enemy trenches. Already pummelled by the blast of the explosions, seared by the heat, showered with gravel and debris, and almost choked by the smoke, they were relieved to be able to leave the courtyard and, spreading out on the move to give themselves a broad arc of fire, zigzag towards what was left of the enemy positions.

What they found was a valley of death in which only a few human souls remained. Scorched though they were, covered with blisters, their bones broken, soaked in their own blood, some of the guerrillas still had the will to fight.

A single shot rang out.

Norton, who had been peering into the blackened remains of the trenches, not thinking for a moment that anyone could still be alive there, suddenly went into a spasm, jerking epileptically, dropped his weapon and let out a strangled moan before flopping face down in the dirt.

'Fuck!' Mad Mike bawled. 'Those bastards are still alive!'

Both enraged and shocked, he fired burst after burst of his M16A1 automatic rifle into the pitiful creatures still twitching in the shell holes, making sure that not a single one of them would ever fire his weapon or throw a grenade again. He was still firing, clearly out of control, when Shagger grabbed him by the shoulders and pulled him away.

'Enough!' Shagger snapped. 'All these bastards are dead.'

'Sergeant Norton!' Mad Mike exclaimed. 'Sergeant Norton! These bastards . . .'

'They're all dead,' Shagger repeated, again shaking Mad Mike furiously. 'There's no more we can do here. Get a grip on yourself, Corporal!'

Eventually, as if coming out of a trance, Mad Mike took half a dozen deep, even breaths and regained control of himself. But even then he looked back at the body of Sergeant Norton, lying face down in the dirt, and said, 'Come on, we've got to . . .'

'No!' Shagger snapped. 'We can't do anything for him. The burial detail will find him later. Let's get back to the village and join up with the others. OK?'

'Yeah. Sorry, Sarge.'

'Good on you! Let's go.'

As they hurried back to the centre of the village they could hear the sound of the battle still raging as fiercely as ever. Reaching the bottom of the hill, they soon saw what was happening.

'Bloody hell!' Red exclaimed.

By now, the VC using the peasants as hostages were ignoring them and were instead trying to flee into the houses on either side of the square. These, however, were already being cleared by the troopers of 1 and 3 Squadrons with a combination of rifles and hand-grenades. As the houses rang with the sound of automatic gunfire and roared with successive grenade explosions, and as whole chunks of wall and windows were blown out and VC bodies, occasionally SAS, fell into the street, the guerrillas hoping to get into the houses were forced to bunch up together in the middle of the square.

Now caught in a four-way crossfire and being brutally cut down, they nevertheless refused to give up and, forming into a rough circle, embarked on a seemingly suicidal fire-fight.

'Christ!' Jimbo exclaimed. 'You've got to admire the little bastards. They're going to slug it out to the last man.'

'And the last man it's going to be,' Dead-eye replied.

He didn't even wait for an order from Callaghan. As was his way, he raced out into the square, firing his SLR from the hip with deadly accuracy, taking out one VC after the other. Inspired by his performance, Shagger, Jimbo, Red and Mad Mike did the same, while Callaghan looked on, at first in amazement and then with a grim smile on his face. When he saw them in the midst of the turmoil, all weaving left and right, crouched low, firing on the move, he raced up to join them.

Within minutes, the fire-fight had become a CQB situation, with many of the SAS men using Browning pistols at close range and some even using their Fairburn-Sykes commando daggers to stab VC lunging at them with machetes. Meanwhile, as the bloody struggle was at its height, the rest of 1 and 3 Squadrons were completing the clearing of the houses on both sides of the square and the 5th and 6th Battalions, led by their tanks and APCs, were closing in to crush the guerrillas making their last-ditch stand.

Eventually, when they reached the VC, the latter, recognizing their fate, threw up their hands. Within minutes, blindfolded and with their hands tied in front of them, they were roped together and led away at gunpoint to the APCs that would transport them back to the FOB. From there they would be flown by Chinooks to the immense POW camp at Nui Dat.

What happened next, in the darkness of night, was to no one's taste, though it was a job that had to be done. As the SAS got on with the dangerous task of checking every house in the village for any remaining VC snipers, the soldiers of 5th and 6th Battalions rounded up the frightened peasants and herded them into the APCs for transportation to a resettlement area. Once there, they would be fed, medically examined, given clothes and other necessaries, then be flown or driven to their allocated resettlement area, where they would help construct a new, fortified village, be trained to defend it themselves, and then helped with the planting of new crops to make them self-sufficient.

When the last of the peasants had been driven away, the captured village was put to the torch and, where necessary, blown up to ensure that it could not be used by the VC in the future. This was, for many of the soldiers and SAS men, an unpleasant and often deeply distressing task, but it could not be avoided. All through the night, as the check for remaining VC snipers continued, the destruction of the houses and other buildings was completed, by explosion or fire, with flames illuminating the darkness and a pall of smoke blotting out the moon and stars.

Adding a surrealistic, even nightmarish appearance to the scene were the USAF Chinooks and RAAF Iroquois which descended through the smoke with spotlights blazing. Having landed, they disgorged medics, stretchers and other basic medical equipment, more ammunition, food and water. Once these were delivered, the same choppers flew out the many wounded and dead, one of whom was SAS Sergeant Norton.

When first light came, it revealed a scene of black, smouldering devastation peopled by dozens of filthy, weary soldiers. Among them were Shagger, Dead-eye, Jimbo, Red and Mad Mike. Crouching together in a circle, they were sharing a welcome brew-up and a smoke.

They had barely taken the first sip when Callaghan approached them.

'There's only one job left to do,' he said.

The men nodded wearily.

15

Though the VC tunnel complex ran under the fake village, its entrances were all located in a cleared area of jungle just outside the settlement. The first task of the SAS was to investigate that area to ensure that none of the VC were still inhabiting the rectangular pits sunk into the ground. They also had to check the area for punji pits and other booby-traps.

The two VC defectors had given the SAS detailed maps of the tunnel system, and these enabled them to locate the sunken pits and punji traps at ground level. As each trooper was given his own copy of the maps, he was able to avoid the punji pits while moving stealthily through the village and checking that the rectangular pits were empty.

Crawling on his belly under one of the sloping thatched roofs raised only a few inches off the ground, Shagger found himself staring down into a complete kitchen, with a kiln-shaped stove covered with pots and pans and bamboo-and-plank shelves laden with eating and drinking utensils. Though the pots and pans were filled with soups or stews simmering on a low heat, there was no sign of anyone in the kitchen.

Shagger then saw, in one corner of the kitchen, beneath the shelves, a closed trapdoor.

Obviously the cook and his helpers had escaped down there, into the tunnel complex, when they realized that the village had been captured.

Turning away, Shagger indicated with a hand signal to those behind him that the pit was empty.

Meanwhile Dead-eye was also crawling on his belly under a low camouflaged roof. Glancing down and preparing to fire his SLR, he saw an empty rectangular pit that contained a scattering of plates, chicken bones and other scraps of food. Used cartridges littered the floor of the pit. Looking more carefully, Dead-eye made out the faint impressions made by guerrillas who had obviously been lying belly down on the sloping sides of the pit, ready to fire their weapons at the approach of an enemy. Realizing that he had come across a firing pit, he checked the defectors' map and noted that this pit also contained one of the concealed entrances to the tunnel complex. Pleased, he used a hand signal to indicate that the pit was empty.

Red had also crawled under one of the artificial roofs, to find himself looking down into a rectangular pit that contained a crude, hand-carved wooden table and chairs, the disconnected wires of what had been a field phone, and a wall of planks – the other walls were of compacted earth – that was covered with pins clearly used to pin up maps and graphs. Checking his map, he decided that he had found the conference chamber. Studying the floor again, he noticed a closed trapdoor exactly where it was indicated on his map. That trapdoor, he knew, led down into a conical air-raid shelter that also served to amplify the sound of approaching aircraft. Below that was the rest of the tunnel complex.

Like the others, Red indicated with his hand that the pit he had found was empty.

Meanwhile Jimbo and Mad Mike had both uncovered concealed trapdoors sunk a few inches into the soft earth and covered with grass and leaves so as to look like part of the flat ground.

When Mad Mike eased open his trapdoor and shone his torch in, the beam illuminated a narrow tunnel that curved away slightly about fifteen feet down. According to his map, it led to the VC sleeping chamber. There was no sign of anyone down there and Mike hand-signalled this fact to the others.

Jimbo, when he opened his trapdoor slightly and poked his torch in, found the beam reflecting off a dark pool of water some fifty feet below. Directing the beam left then right, he saw the circular walls of a well. Moving it upwards until it lit up an area about twenty-five feet higher, or halfway down the well, he saw what appeared to be two tunnels facing each other, one raised slightly higher than the other. Studying them more intently, he thought he could discern ridges cut out of the wall facing the lower tunnel. These, he surmised, could have been used as footholds for someone straddling the well – one foot on the floor of the passageway, the other on the ridge – to enable them to lower a bucket on a rope to the water-table. Admiring the cleverness of his enemy, Jimbo turned away from the trapdoor and used a hand signal to indicate that the well was clear and he was ready to go.

Callaghan was crouching with three SAS troopers under the trees beyond the perimeter of the village, by the three hidden smoke outlets from the kitchen, one trooper guarding each outlet to ensure that no VC tried escaping through them. Seeing his men's final hand signal, from Jimbo, Callaghan raised and sharply dropped his own hand, indicating that the attack was to commence.

Dead-eye was the first down. Like the others, he was armed only with a torch, his 9mm Browning High Power handgun, his dagger, M26 high-explosive hand-grenades, and an unusual amount of spare ammunition. After dragging the heavy, camouflaged covering slightly to the side, he jumped down into the sunken pit of the firing post, his boots cracking some of the plates left on the floor. Kicking chicken bones and spent cartridges aside, he made his way to the trapdoor half hidden behind some packing crates. Kneeling down, and with his Browning in his right hand, the safety-catch already off, he carefully raised the trapdoor a little and glanced down.

The tunnel below was narrow, very dark and ran almost horizontally away from him. Gingerly sticking his head down the hole, Dead-eye thought he saw a few strands of pale light where the tunnel appeared to curve up again towards the surface.

Neither seeing nor hearing signs of movement, he carefully lowered himself into the tunnel until he was on his hands and knees. As in that position his back was still scraping the top of the tunnel, even he, who had bravely suffered every kind of horror and danger in the past, could not help but feel an overwhelming claustrophobia.

Frequently, he heard the soft scuffling of rats.

Taking a deep breath, then letting it out slowly, he turned on his torch, holding it in his left hand, gripped the Browning in his right, and began the slow crawl along the roughly horizontal tunnel. He had travelled only ten yards in as many minutes and was breaking out in a sweat, when he came to a spot where the tunnel started curving back up to the surface and rays of pale light beamed back down. Straining to see upwards, Dead-eye thought he could make out a square shape outlined by light. He was looking up at another trapdoor exit.

Realizing that the tunnel was unlikely to curve down and up from one trapdoor exit to another, but must surely go down deeper into the system, Dead-eye shone his torch on the floor directly in front of him. He saw what appeared to be a square-shaped portion of soil slightly raised above the rest of the floor of the tunnel. Wiping the sweat from his eyes, he inched forward to it, placed the torch on the floor, and very carefully groped around with his fingers, eventually finding what felt like the underside of a wooden trapdoor. Lifting it very slowly, fearful of booby-traps, he peered down and saw only another dark tunnel, this one curving away at a forty-five-degree angle.

There was no light of any kind, nor any sound of movement.

Aiming the torch down, Dead-eye saw the tunnel more clearly curving away out of sight. Pulling the trapdoor from the opening, he lowered himself in, found himself sliding dangerously down an almost vertical section, but came to rest when the tunnel started levelling out. He rolled over on to his belly, raised himself on to his hands and knees, then crawled forward as best he could, still holding the torch in his left hand, but keeping it aimed just a few feet in front of him in case the VC should see it, and holding the Browning in his right.

Gradually, as he inched forward, frequently tapping the ground ahead with the barrel of the gun to check for a trapdoor concealing a punji pit, the fetid air changed into something cleaner, cooler and he sensed, rather than saw, a similar, almost imperceptible brightening in the darkness ahead.

Crawling on, along a steep incline, he eventually reached a point where the tunnel levelled out and led into a large, empty space that looked like a natural cave but had, just like the tunnels, been hacked out by human hand.

Checking the ground directly in front of him, he noticed a pale, circular-shaped pool of light. Crawling forward to it, he saw that the light was beaming up along a particularly narrow tunnel – certainly too small for a human to pass through – which sloped down at forty-five degrees. When he squinted along it, he saw an even brighter light and thought he heard the murmur of many voices.

Straightening up as best he could, Dead-eye checked his copy of the defectors' map with his torch and concluded that he was almost certainly at the air vent leading up from the underground forward aid station for the wounded. About a yard further on from the vent was another trapdoor camou-flaged with the same mud as on the tunnel floor. That, Dead-eye knew, was the entrance and exit to the forward aid station.

Shining his torch beyond that trapdoor, to the far side of the empty cavern, he saw a raised portion of the floor which he assumed was another trapdoor. According to the map, it was one of the blast, gas and waterproof trapdoors sited at each end of a U-shaped tunnel drop that acted as a blast wall. Shining the torch to the left of that trapdoor, but much higher up, Dead-eye saw a tunnel heading upwards in the opposite direction and stopping at yet another trapdoor. This one, he knew, led up to the sleeping chamber, which, apart from containing many VC at all times, had a tunnel at its far end, leading up to the concealed trapdoor entrance that Red had been designated to enter.

Assuming that no VC were likely to emerge from the blast, gas and waterproof trapdoor nearby, but that a loud noise would almost certainly bring a horde of guerrillas along the tunnel leading down from the sleeping chamber into the cavern, Dead-eye realized he would have to be quick.

After crawling forward to the air vent, he unclipped two hand-grenades, released the pins and dropped the grenades down the air vent, into the forward aid station. Even as they were rolling down, he crawled across the vent and went up to the entrance-exit trapdoor. He had just reached it when the grenades exploded with a muffled roar, followed by the terrible screaming of men scorched by heat, pummelled by the blast, and lacerated by flying, red-hot metal.

The screams were followed instantly by the high-pitched chattering and shouting of the surviving VC, then by the sounds of colliding weapons.

Lying flat out on his belly and holding his Browning in both hands, Dead-eye aimed at the entrance-exit trapdoor. When it opened, the head and shoulders of a VC appeared through the hole. Dead-eye fired once, putting a bullet right between the guerrilla's eyes. Even as the man was dropping back down through the hole, falling on top of those jabbering excitedly below him, Dead-eye crawled forward, dropped another grenade down through the hole, then slammed the trapdoor shut and rolled away from it.

This time the explosion was much louder and was again accompanied by terrible screaming. When Dead-eye opened the trapdoor again and looked down, he saw a pile of dead bodies at the bottom of the tunnel, illuminated eerily by a light beaming out of the smoking forward aid station.

Though he could hear the groans and occasional screams of the badly wounded, he knew that no one could have remained undamaged from that last grenade and that an attack from down there was now unlikely.

Slamming the trapdoor shut again to keep the smoke in, and aware that it would probably choke the wounded to death, Dead-eye turned away just as another muffled explosion rose from the far side of the empty cavern, up where the sleeping chamber was located. This was followed by a single, sustained scream so terrible that it blotted out the bawling of the men in the sleeping chamber.

With that chilling sound reverberating in his head, Dead-eye crawled through the darkness, lighting his way with the torch, until he reached the blast, gas and waterproof trapdoor. Lying there on his belly, still haunted by that terrible screaming, he switched off the torch, plunging the cavern into almost total darkness, and aimed his Browning at the tunnel leading down in a lazy curve from the sleeping chamber.

The agonized cries of the wounded man continued unabated.

It was Mad Mike who was screaming. Knowing from his map that the concealed trapdoor entrance to the sleeping chamber was almost perpendicular, sloping only slightly, and levelled out at the bottom over a camouflaged punji pit located between the tunnel and the sleeping chamber, Mike had raised the trapdoor and lowered himself down into the tunnel with extreme care, holding his thumb on the pin of the grenade in his left hand.

Though the tunnel was almost perpendicular, its circular wall had many man-made grooves which provided a tenuous hold for feet and hands; but holding the grenade, Mike had considerable difficulty in maintaining his balance and soon found himself sweating, not only from the suffocating heat and stench, but also from tension.

His intention was to climb down as closely as possible to the concealed trapdoor of the punji pit, then roll a couple of grenades over it, into the sleeping chamber. He would then dispatch the few survivors with his Browning, possibly following up with another grenade.

However, when he was only halfway down, the soil that formed the lip of one of the man-made grooves had come away in his hand and he felt himself falling backwards. Desperately using both hands to get a grip on something, he let the grenade go and it rolled down around the bend, where the tunnel levelled out, then across the trapdoor of the punji pit and on into the crowded sleeping chamber.

Mike had just managed to grab the lip of another groove and was desperately battling to regain his balance and position flat against the wall when the grenade exploded among the sleeping guerrillas.

Stunned by the noise, which reverberated dreadfully in the narrow tunnel, Mike lost first his grip, then his footing, fell backwards against the opposite wall, and slid down the tunnel.

Knowing exactly what was going to happen to him, he filled up with a blinding, heart-stopping fear and let out a strangled groan before falling on to the trapdoor, which tilted down under his weight and sent him plunging backwards on to the bed of poison and excrement-smeared, razor-sharp stakes in a pit of pitch darkness.

Pierced through his legs, arms and back, though his neck and head were missed, Mike spasmed relentlessly, helplessly, soaked in his own blood, blinded by it, choking on it, then released a long-drawn-out scream that blotted out the screaming of the VC in the sleeping chamber and seemed to him to reverberate for ever.

In fact, it was over quickly. Some of the surviving VC rushed out of the smoke-filled sleeping chamber and stopped at the lip of the booby-trap. Seeing that blood-soaked figure screaming in agony below them, and aware that he was the one who had killed or wounded so many of their comrades, they angrily emptied the magazines of their AK47s into him, making him spasm even more violently, blowing the stakes to pieces all around him, turning him into bloody flesh and bone, and finally – though they had not intended this – putting him out of his misery.

Unable to cross the punji pit, and having already heard the explosion from the direction of the forward aid station, the VC who had survived the grenade explosion in the sleeping chamber made their way back through the devastation, stepping over the groaning wounded and the bodies of their dead comrades, to raise the trapdoor and crawl one by one down the tunnel that led into the empty cavern containing the entrance to the forward aid station.

Waiting for them in the high-ceilinged cavern, Dead-eye saw them illuminated in the light pouring down the tunnel from the sleeping chamber. Knowing that if he shot the first man crawling out, the others might take another route to him, he waited until all five of them had crawled out before straightening up briefly and lobbing the grenade he had been holding in his hand. Even as it was arcing through the air, he dropped back down, stretched out on his belly and aimed his Browning two-handed at the guerrillas.

The sound of the exploding grenade was amplified tremendously in the large cavern and the group of VC were bowled over in all directions. Two remained where they had fallen, in the swirling smoke; one rolled on to his belly, badly wounded but still determined to fight; and the other two managed to get to their knees and aim their AK47s directly at Dead-eye.

They were too late. Dead-eye fired two shots, one at each man, and was already aiming at the wounded man before the other two fell. The wounded man managed to get off one shot, but weakened by loss of blood he couldn't hold the weapon steady and the bullet ricocheted off the wall high above Dead-eye's head. Dead-eye's third shot blew the man's brains out. All five men were dead.

Hearing another explosion, Dead-eye hurried over to the blast, gas and waterproof trapdoor, raised it, looked in, then carefully lowered himself down and began the arduous crawl along the narrow tunnel that led up to the conical air-raid shelter.

A whiff of smoke drifted down to him.

At the signal from Callaghan, Red lowered himself down into the rectangular pit shown on his map as the conference chamber. He had learnt from that same map that the trapdoor in the far-left-hand corner of that chamber led down, via a short, L-shaped tunnel, to the conical air-raid shelter.

Instead of going straight into the tunnel, Red spent some time examining the conference chamber and found some potentially useful maps and graphs curled up on the floor under the crude wooden table.

Satisfied that there was not much else of value, he went to the trapdoor and gently raised it with his left hand, holding his Browning in his right. There was enough light in the conference chamber to let him see most of the way down the unusually short tunnel before it curved out of sight to the right.

Leaning further forward, Red put his head sideways over the hole and listened with his left ear. Convinced he could hear the murmuring of voices, therefore certain that the air-raid shelter was not only inhabited but was just around that bend about six feet down – too close for comfort – Red lowered the trapdoor again.

Aware from the map that there was a very narrow air vent running from the ground a few feet east of the conference chamber, down into the air-raid shelter, Red clambered out of the eastern side of the pit and went over to the concealed air vent. After removing the grass and leaves sprinkled over the flat, wooden cover, he removed the grille of the vent itself and stuck his ear to the hole. Again, but more distinctly, he heard the sound of murmuring from below.

Satisfied, he unclipped a grenade from his belt, released the pin, dropped the grenade into the vent, then rolled aside as fast as he could. He had just stopped rolling when he heard the muffled explosion from below, followed by screaming, then silence. He sprang to his feet, ran back to the rectangular pit, jumped down into the conference chamber and hurried back over to the trapdoor. Opening it, he smelt the smoke of the explosion drifting upwards, but heard no sound of movement from within.

Carefully lowering himself into the smoky darkness of the almost vertical tunnel, he practically slid down the rest of the way and almost became jammed in the sharp bend at the bottom. Realizing that it was wide enough for only the smallest of men, which he wasn't, he almost panicked, but eventually he managed to wriggle free and, having no other option, crawled backwards, his rectum tightening with the expectation of a bullet, into the smoke-filled air-raid shelter.

It was indeed conical and claustrophobically small. It also contained the bodies of two VC soldiers, both of whom had been badly scorched and slashed to ribbons.

Choking on the smoke, Red hurriedly raised the trapdoor in the floor, glanced in, saw nothing but the smoke that was escaping from the shelter, and carefully lowered himself down.

Again, it was an almost vertical tunnel, but it dropped only about six feet before turning right. Aware that even on hands and knees his back was scraping the top of the tunnel, and slightly unnerved by the almost total darkness, Red started sweating and then remembered to turn on his torch. Holding it awkwardly in one hand, tapping the ground ahead with the barrel of his Browning to check for booby-traps, and still sweating profusely, he made his way slowly along the tunnel until he came to a trapdoor located just before a dead-end.

With no other choice but to continue down even deeper into the tunnel complex – particularly since the smoke from the air-raid shelter was following him and starting to blind and choke him – Red tentatively raised the trapdoor and peered into the tunnel below.

He saw a pair of eyes staring up at him from behind the barrel of an automatic rifle.

It was Dead-eye.

'What the hell are you doing here?' Dead-eye whispered.

'I was going to make my way down as far as I could go,' Red replied, beginning to shake with the release of tension.

'I've cleared it all out down there,' Dead-eye told him, studying the tunnel Red had just come along. 'According to my map, if we go back in that direction, passing the vertical tunnel you just came down, we'll end up at the well. Let's see what's down there.'

Pouring sweat, breathing too deeply for comfort, Red nodded.

'OK,' he said. 'Only problem is, there's no room to turn in this tunnel, so I'll have to crawl backwards the whole way.'

'That way you might get a bullet up the arse,' Dead-eye told him. 'Look, I'm going to lower myself back down into this vertical tunnel – it's only six feet down to where it turns. When I'm at the bottom, you crawl across the trapdoor opening to the dead-end, then lower your legs into this hole. When you've done that, you can turn around and crawl out facing the way you've just come.'

'You beaut!' Red exclaimed.

They did just that: Dead-eye dropped to the bottom of his hole; Red crawled across it, lay belly down with his legs dangling down into it, turned around laboriously by clinging to the rim of the hole, and finally pulled himself back up on to the floor of the tunnel, back on to his hands and knees, but now facing in the right direction. When he moved off, shining his torch straight ahead, Dead-eye pulled himself up out of the vertical tunnel and followed him, also on hands and knees.

The two men advanced painfully along the tunnel, heading for the well. When they reached it, they found that the tunnel ended in the middle of the well, about twenty-five feet above the water-table, with another twenty-five up to the surface.

The bodies of two dead VC soldiers were sinking, one on top of the other, into the bloodied water below.

A rope had been slung from a rotating pole mounted between two Y-shaped uprights placed on two sides of the mouth of the well. The rope was now dangling free. At the opposite side of the well, but slightly higher than they were, was another tunnel.

From its dark mouth, a pair of eyes were staring at them.

They were Jimbo's.

After waving at them, Jimbo silently pointed directly below him with his index finger, indicating a deep groove that had been hacked out of the wall opposite the tunnel where Dead-eye and Red were kneeling. It was clear to both men that he meant they were to use it as a foothold.

'You mean we've got to straddle the two sides with both feet,' Red whispered, being out in front of Dead-eye, 'and then somehow swing around, grab the rope, pull ourselves up that couple of feet, and then swing ourselves into your tunnel?'

'That's right,' Jimbo replied. 'When you reach me, I'll grab you and haul you in.'

'I can't do that, mate,' Red said. 'I'm not claustrophobic – I've been down enough tunnels – but I've no head for heights.'

'Bullshit!' Jimbo retorted. 'I did it. And if I did it, you can.'

In fact, Jimbo was lying. He had not been forced to straddle the opposite sides of the circular wall. Instead, having been lowered into the top half of the well by rope, he had simply swung himself sideways and then thrown himself into the tunnel. But he knew that he would not help Red by telling him this.

'Turn towards me,' Jimbo whispered. 'Then stretch out your right leg until your foot's resting in that groove. Keep your other foot on the floor of the tunnel. Without any delay or hesitation, you then swing your left foot off the floor of the tunnel, twist your body towards this wall, and reach up and grab hold of the rope. When you've done that, haul yourself up three feet, then kick the opposite wall to make yourself swing in my direction. Don't worry, I'll grab you.'

As the mouths of both tunnels widened enough to enable an average-sized man to stand upright, it was obvious that the fearless VC had done something similar to cross from one tunnel to the next. Knowing this, Red had no choice but to clip his torch back on to his belt, holster his Browning, stand upright, straddle the narrow well directly above the two dead bodies in the water twenty-five feet below, then swing his left foot off the edge of the tunnel and grab for the rope.

He made it.

Dangling there, all that distance above the two dead VC, he almost blacked out with panic, but somehow managed to stay in control and gradually, painfully, hauled himself up until he was level with the floor of Jimbo's tunnel. Once there, he twisted around until his back was to Jimbo, raised his legs, pressed his feet against the wall, then pushed hard until he was swinging backwards. Flying into the wide mouth of the tunnel, into that dreadful darkness, he felt Jimbo's hands grabbing him and hauling him down to the ground. He was lying there, sprawled on top of Jimbo, when the rope sailed back out into the narrow well.

Breathing deeply, but immensely relieved, Red sat upright, then wriggled away to enable Jimbo to take up his original position at the mouth of the tunnel. When he did so, Dead-eye repeated Red's dangerous, acrobatic performance and was soon swinging backwards into Jimbo's embrace. Hauled in, he fell between the two men, then let the rope go.

Crawling to the edge of the tunnel, Dead-eye glanced down at the two guerrillas floating in the water, then turned back to Jimbo and asked, 'What happened?'

Jimbo shrugged. 'We rigged up this bucket-lowering contraption – like the well originally had – to lower me down, using the coiled rope as a stirrup for one foot. I was just above this tunnel – which, as you now know, is higher than the other – when one of those bastards came out of your tunnel, luckily with his back turned towards me. Stripped to the waist, he straddled the two sides of the wall and started lowering a bucket on a rope, obviously intending to collect water for his mates. So dangling there, directly above him, with my foot in the stirrup and holding the rope with one hand, I unholstered my nine-milly with the other and shot him through the top of the head. His head turned into a fucking pomegranate and he fell down through the well, into the water below.'

Jimbo grinned, clearly relishing his feat, before continuing. 'Two seconds later, his mate stuck his head out, looking up, not believing his bleeding eyes, and I got in a neat double-tap, popping him in the head, and he staggered about a bit, wondering where his head had gone, then fell off the edge of the tunnel and plunged into the water, right on top of his mate. I hung there a bit longer, waiting for more of the fuckers to materialize, and when they didn't, I swung myself on to here. I was just about to head off along this tunnel when I heard you two coming. Of course, I didn't know it was you – I thought it was Charlie – so you don't know how close you came to taking your last breath.'

Red grinned and shook his head from side to side. 'Jesus H. Christ!' he whispered.

'Where's Shagger?' Dead-eye asked.

'He went down through the kitchen,' Red told him, 'to try to find the connecting tunnel to the rest of the system. Apparently this system runs for miles – not just under this village, but under a hell of a lot more. Shagger wants to locate that connecting tunnel and block it, to stop the VC linking up again. We were hoping to meet up.'

'Where's the tunnel lead to?' Dead-eye asked.

'According to the map, down to a storage cache for weapons, explosives and rice. It's not on the map, but the defectors had reason to suspect that a passage leads from there to the connecting passage, which is used as a kind of supply route.'

'Then let's go,' Dead-eye said.

With Dead-eye in the lead, shining his dipped torch, they all crawled on their hands and knees along the dark, dank tunnel. After about ten minutes, when Red and even Jimbo were beginning to imagine fearfully that they were in a dead-end and might be trapped there for ever – buried alive, as it were, in this foul-smelling, pitch-black hole – they came to another trapdoor.

After giving a hand signal to indicate that the others should stay still and remain silent, Dead-eye switched off his torch, plunging them all into a terrifying, total darkness, then raised the trapdoor an inch. As he did so, light beamed up out of the tunnel. Peering through the slit between the trapdoor and the ground, Dead-eye saw a vertical tunnel of about five feet dropping down to a pile of packing crates, racks of weapons and boxes of rice. Raising the trapdoor a little higher, he heard the sound of boxes being moved about and of high-pitched Vietnamese conversation. It then dawned on him that they were now so far away from the rest of the complex that the VC down there probably still didn't know about the battle that had been fought in the other tunnels.

Not knowing exactly what was down there other than the supplies and the workers in charge of them, Dead-eye realized it would be foolish to just drop in and decided instead to throw in two grenades, then go in with the other men at the height of the commotion.

He had just unclipped two grenades from his belt and was releasing the pins when four loud explosions – almost certainly hand-grenades – occurred one after the other in quick succession, followed by much screaming and shouting.

Instantly, Dead-eye released the pins from his own two grenades and dropped them into the tunnel, right on top of the wooden crates directly below.

'Get down!' he bawled.

Although he and the other men were already on hands and knees, they dropped to their bellies, pressed their faces to the earth, and covered their ears with their hands.

The explosion was so noisy, so fierce, with flames even spitting up through the trapdoor near where Dead-eye was lying, that it could not possibly have been caused by two grenades alone. Then, when Dead-eye heard another explosion, then another, he realized that the grenades had set off the crates of explosive and ammunition, each explosion triggering another with devastating results.

Dead-eye lay near the trapdoor, pressing his face in the dirt, covering his ears with his hands, but still feeling the fierce heat coming up out of the tunnel and hearing the noise, despite blocking his ears. Eventually, however, the explosions tapered away and, when Dead-eye removed his hands, all he could hear were the moans and groans of the wounded.

'Let's go!' he snapped.

Crawling to the edge of the hole, he pulled himself to the other side until he was able to bend from the stomach down, with his legs dangling into the hole. When he was in that position, he unholstered his Browning, took the torch in his other hand, and let himself drop down through the tunnel.

Landing in the scorched debris of the exploded ammunition crates, sending expended shells clattering with each step he took, he turned around, saw only pitch-darkness, heard the moaning and groaning of the wounded on the floor, then finally switched on his torch, tensing himself for a VC bullet.

No bullet came. Instead, while the others dropped down through the tunnel behind him, also making a metallic racket as they trampled on expended shells, he saw in the beam of his torch the awesome devastation caused by the many explosions, with blistered, lacerated, bloody VC writhing and moaning amid pieces of blackened wood, bent nails, smashed weapons, piles of rice, lazily drifting dust, and a general stench of scorched human flesh, urine, excrement, cordite, burning wood and acrid smoke. Here and there, in the darkness, blue and yellow flames flickered eerily.

Suddenly, from that ghastly darkness filled with cries of human pain, Dead-eye's torch picked out a pair of human eyes staring along the barrel of an automatic rifle.

When the barrel was lowered, Dead-eye recognized Shagger.

In search of the connecting tunnel to the rest of the system, Shagger had gone down into the tunnel of the kitchen in its rectangular pit at ground level, followed it around for a good twenty minutes to a false tunnel with a dead-end, then was forced to go all the way back, backwards on his hands and knees. After checking his obviously outdated map, he had taken another tunnel which offered more hope because it was lined with camouflaged trapdoors and – as Shagger found out more than once when he tapped the ground ahead with the barrel of his Browning – more than one deadly punji pit.

Knowing that he could not place any weight on either end of the punji pits' tilting lids, he had only been able to cross those he came to by throwing himself from his hands-and-knees posture directly on to the lid with his weight spread equidistant across it, midriff on the lid, hands on one side, feet on the other, and then inching slowly across to prevent the lid from tilting. Though this was effective, it took a tremendous amount of time and was extremely exhausting.

Eventually reaching another trapdoor that led into a descending tunnel, Shagger had slithered down into it, crawled along it, and finally came to another tunnel that linked it up with what – as he knew from his study of the VC map – could only have been the storage cache for weapons, explosives and rice.

Aware of this fact, he accepted that the tunnel he had found was the supply route to the other villages – the underground route he had been seeking.

Determined to destroy the storage cache and then arrange for another SAS sapper team to come down and block the connecting tunnel by laying delayed-timer explosives that would fill it with rubble, Shagger had rolled four hand-grenades, one after the other, down the tunnel, into the storage cache.

It was those explosions that Dead-eye had heard just before he sent down his own.

Now all of them, with the exception of the unfortunate Mad Mike, had met up in the destroyed storage cache.

They had put the VC tunnel complex out of action.

After emotionally shaking hands, they crawled into one of the tunnels and made their way back to the surface, glad to see the light of day.

16

Shortly after the SAS men emerged from the tunnel complex, the remote smoke outlets from the kitchen were filled in with cement, to prevent smoke from escaping, then air blowers were used to force smoke through the trapdoors in the rectangular pits down into the tunnels, filling them with smoke and forcing out the last of the VC.

That other wounded VC may have been choked to death was an issue not widely discussed.

For the next three days, when the last of the VC had emerged and the smoke had cleared, the SAS men continued to search the complex and gradually discovered that it had contained a major VC headquarters hidden underground in a multi-level labyrinth covering a total area of approximately two square miles. The artificial village on top had been used as the living quarters and recreation area for the huge command post below, with the underground sleeping chamber used only for those on duty at any given time. Many weapons, including six 12.7mm anti-aircraft machine-guns, and more than 100,000 pages of invaluable documents, were uncovered during the next few days.

When it had been confirmed by the tunnel rats that every last VC had either been captured or killed, the connecting tunnel to the other tunnel complexes was filled with high explosive, which, when detonated by a timer device from the surface, filled the tunnel with densely packed rubble that would have been almost impossible to remove. The tunnel – and the VC supply route to the other underground tunnel complexes – was therefore blocked for good.

With this major job completed, as much as possible of the complex was destroyed and what was left was contaminated with crystallized CS tear-gas.

According to figures calculated from the actions taken at both the nearby village and the tunnel complex, 130 Viet Cong were killed, ninety-five were taken prisoner, and 509 suspects were rounded up for questioning. The Australian casualties were seven dead and twenty-three wounded.

By the time the operation had been completed, Lieutenant-Colonel Callaghan, Dead-eye and Jimbo had forged a strong friendship with the Australian 1 and 3 SAS Squadrons, based on mutual admiration and respect. The three men from 22 SAS stayed on in Vietnam for another month, taking part in other actions against the VC, including reconnaissance and more 'tunnel rat' operations. By the end of that month, they had learnt a lot about the enemy, about the Australian SAS, and about counter-insurgency operations in general.

Shortly after coming home, Lieutenant-Colonel Callaghan was returned to his original unit, 3 Commando, retired from active service, and assigned to a desk job in 3 Commando's Intelligence and Planning Department, where he put what he had learnt in Vietnam and elsewhere to good use.

Back in Hereford, Dead-eye and Jimbo kept in touch with Shagger and Red, swapping tall tales, insults and some more serious thoughts in regular letters. This correspondence ended abruptly seven months later. Dead-eye and Jimbo learnt that the two Aussies had been killed in the notorious multi-layered labyrinth of tunnels that centred on Cu Chi near Saigon and stretched as far as the Cambodian border.

Jimbo was sent back to the Radfan in 1967 to help cover the British withdrawal from Aden. On his return he was retired from active duty and transferred to the Training Wing, Hereford, as a reluctant member of the Directing Staff of 22 SAS.

Dead-eye, the youngest of the three SAS men, went on to serve in Belfast in 1976, then he too became a member of the Directing Staff. By that time, his old friend Jimbo, a victim of the passing years, had been retired completely from the service.

An era had ended.